The CAVE to Another World

The CAVE to Another World

TOBIAS MALM

First paperback edition Februari 2023

ISBN 978-91-527-5668-3 (paperback)
ISBN 978-91-527-5669-0 (ebook)

Published by Tobias Malm

www.tobiasmalm.com

PREFACE

ABOUT THREE YEARS AGO, the halls of the Sorbonne buzzed with rumors regarding the sudden disappearance of two promising exchange students. I had the opportunity to supervise one of them, Alexander Conway, and was thus the first to express concerns about their unexpected departure from our institution. His peer in this mystery was the younger Abasi Hamisi, a student I had met only in my lectures, but whose potential was clear. Alexander had been deeply immersed in his doctoral thesis on the sex-based division of labor among Homo neanderthalensis—a subject he approached with intense passion. So, when he didn't return after the summer break, I sensed something was wrong. Efforts to reach both young men were unsuccessful. Learning that they hadn't returned home, their families, informed of their absence from the Sorbonne, reported them missing.

Speculation started circulating among the students that the two had embarked on a summer journey together, but their destination remained unknown. It wasn't until a month later that authorities were able to trace their last known location to the enigmatic Białowieża Forest in Poland. However, the purpose behind their journey continued to be shrouded in mystery.

Every investigative path reached a dead end within the dense, secluded confines of the forest, and after a year of relentless search without any solid evidence, they were, regrettably, presumed dead, likely victims of the harsh, unforgiving elements during what was assumed to be a misguided adventure in the wilderness. It was against this grim background that a letter, signed by Abasi, landed at my doorstep.

Eagerly, I unfolded the letter, hoping for some clarity. However, to my disappointment, the numerous pages inside seemed more like speculative fiction than a factual account of events. At first, I thought I might be the victim of a cruel joke or perhaps an elaborate hoax created by someone involved in their mysterious disappearance. Another troubling thought also crossed my mind—had Abasi lost touch with reality? Yet, just a few days after receiving this perplexing letter, an unexpected package arrived, forcing me to reconsider the seriousness of its contents.

Inside the package was a remarkably well-preserved skull. Verifying it as a genuine artifact took considerable time, but once its authenticity was confirmed, the previous letter could no longer be dismissed as mere imagination. Creating such a perfect replica would have been nearly impossible.

Following this discovery, I sent a response to Abasi. It took an entire year before I heard back from him, a year filled with growing apprehension and fear for his well-being. Unfortunately, his second letter came without a return address, eliminating any chance for immediate correspondence on my part. I have included both Abasi's accounts and my response here. I believe it is crucial, indeed essential, that this narrative be brought into public discussion—presented here with only minor changes to formatting for readability.

Nathalie Delsarte

THE FIRST LETTER

Hajnówka, Oct. 11th, 20-

Dear Prof. Delsarte,

I'm writing to you concerning Alexander's and my absence from the university. I want you to know that neither of us left out of a lack of interest or respect. Quite the contrary, as you'll soon gather. Nevertheless, I sincerely regret the abruptness of our leaving, and I'm confident Alexander would echo this sentiment, were he here. I ought to have reached out sooner; however, I've grappled with how to articulate what we experienced. It's not just that the tale is difficult to put into words, it's that it revives memories too painful for me to bear. Still, it's crucial that I inform you, both out of respect for your concern about our fates and because I urgently require your counsel. I know my story will be difficult to believe—maybe even impossible. However, I trust the evidence I dispatched alongside this letter has reached you by now. Hopefully, it's enough to convince you to at least consider the possibility that the tale within these pages is true.

To delve into the heart of the matter: two years ago, Alexander confided in me about a profound restlessness with his Ph.D. thesis. He was in a rut, experiencing a sense of stagnation that was all too palpable. Academia seemed to stifle his true calling; he yearned for tangible exploration. He wished to immerse his hands in the earth, excavate new sites, and unearth novel findings, not merely study discoveries made by others from the confines of a lab or an office. It wasn't that he didn't value the field studies we had undertaken. In fact, he relished the exploration of the cave systems in Regourdou, and felt privileged to study the parietal art and remains from the Paleolithic era in the region. However, the majority of our time was spent indoors. For an adventurer like Alexander, this was an unsettling reality. He craved the outdoors, the thrill of the unknown. His frustration with the indoor nature of academia grew to a point where he couldn't bear spending his days buried in books and journals. This impatience was one of the key motivations behind his proposition for us to embark on a camping trip to the Białowieża Forest during our summer break.

Our decision to explore the northern half of Poland was unconventional considering most prehistoric findings were concentrated in the country's southern regions. Yet, we reasoned that even if our explorations proved fruitless—which was a likely outcome—the journey would still be an enriching experience. After all, venturing into the Białowieża Forest, one of the last and largest vestiges of the primeval forest that once sprawled across the European Plain, was akin to stepping back into prehistoric times. Furthermore, the region's relative obscurity compared to other more explored places offered an intriguing possibility; should we uncover anything, it might well be a discovery untouched by others. However, two significant hurdles deterred exploration in this region. First, stringent regulations designed to protect the natural heritage within the forest and its surrounding reserves presented near-insurmountable obstacles to conducting excavations. Second, the dense trees and the thick litter blanketing the ground complicated the task of detecting signs of prehistoric human habitation.

The first issue wasn't unmanageable. Our intent wasn't to embark on large-scale excavations but to engage in discreet exploration, a task we hoped to achieve by navigating the forest clandestinely. The second issue, however, was something we had to accept as it was beyond our control. Personally, it didn't vex me much. I wasn't necessarily expecting us to unearth anything of note; for me, the thrill of traversing one of the world's most captivating landscapes was enough. Alexander, though, harbored a flicker of concern over this challenge. Yet, he clung to optimism, trusting his keen eye wouldn't fail him, as it had rarely done so in the past.

We planned on staying in the forest for about two weeks and packed our bags accordingly. Aside from standard camping equipment—such as a tent and a camping stove—we also brought excavation tools, climbing gear, and caving equipment. We weren't counting on getting any use out of these special accessories, but we brought them along just in case.

We arrived in mid-August, during what was turning out to be Europe's warmest summer on record, with no respite in sight. Yet, the sweltering heat was a small price to pay for the spectacle that was the Białowieża Forest—it was as breathtaking as we had imagined. The thrill of our experience was amplified by our covert entrance; hiking off-road allowed us to sidestep crowds and experience this vast, untouched forest through the lens of explorers, rather than mere tourists.

During our first week, we traversed substantial terrain, navigating meandering rivers lined by ancient bogs. Centuries-old gnarly trees reached for the sky above us, and moss, ferns, and flowers covered the fertile, leafy ground. The smell of decaying wood being slowly devoured by millions of insects and the scent of wildflowers gave rise to a strange sense of tranquility. Alexander didn't voice it, but I sensed he shared this feeling.

As we reached the week's end, our awe for the surroundings hadn't dulled. We watched in awe as a three-toed woodpecker soared from the top of a young pedunculate oak, alighting on a poplar branch mere feet from us. A few moments later, we halted to admire a troop of European bison thundering across a glade framed by a cluster of black alder trees. We cautiously held back until the last echo of their departure faded before advancing into the vacated clearing. I found myself gazing at the azure sky, the symphony of birdsong coaxing my mind into an imagined prehistoric era. The illusion was only broken by the sight of an airplane cutting through the sky at 33,000 feet.

"You can't escape it," Alexander said, a note of resignation in his voice. "Civilization, I mean."

I wiped the sweat from my brow, nodding in agreement. "We are everywhere, aren't we? Like mold consuming an apple."

As night fell, we pitched our camp in the clearing and began planning our course under a blanket of emerging stars. Alexander, his exploratory zeal undiminished, indicated a series of hills to the southwest. "Look here," he urged, shifting the map in my direction. "These hills enclose a small tract of land." His finger traced the perimeter of the isolated area. "It's like a hidden valley, cut off from the rest of the forest. I say we go there!"

I scrutinized the area, a hint of reluctance in my voice. "The terrain seems challenging, perhaps even inaccessible."

Alexander laughed. "You make it sound like that's a bad thing! It's precisely the reason why I think we ought to go there. Very few people probably have."

I was already tired from walking so much in the heat and would have preferred a less grueling route through the forest. However, when I saw the excitement in my friend's eyes and the determination on his face, I couldn't bring myself to object. And thus, the very next day, we began walking toward the hills. It took us half a day to reach the small valley between them, and most of the time was spent finding a safe passage down.

The moss was slippery, and the hillsides were steep and overrun with vegetation. We had to rely on some of our climbing gear to maintain our footing. The skeletal remains of a deer wedged between rocks served as a stark testament to the site's inaccessibility, underscoring the infrequency of its visitors— humans or animals alike. Our descent proved as challenging as I had feared, but the valley rewarded our effort. The ancient forest was even denser here, only letting the occasional sunbeam through the thick canopy above. It was dead silent; not even the birds were singing. All we could hear were our footsteps crunching down on the age-old undergrowth.

We didn't say a word as we carefully walked toward the center of this natural sanctuary. It was harmonious, yet in some abstruse way, uncanny. The narrow valley was permeated by a strange, paradoxical, ambiance. It was pure nature yet unnatural, teeming with life yet abandoned by the living. Navigating these grounds gave rise to a bloodcurdling sensation of being trapped between two extremes, but I could not say what they were. Perhaps right and wrong, order and chaos, or the known and the unknown. Or maybe even life and death. All I knew for sure was that we both had the same feeling of having entered an everlasting twilight beneath the emerald ceiling of this living, desolate cathedral.

The silence was finally broken by Alexander. "Some of these oaks must be centuries old," he mused. "Just consider the marvel of it! These majestic trees have been growing undisturbed throughout modern history. Picture all the events they've lived through—the Thirty Years' War, the French Revolution, the rise and fall of European imperialism, the World Wars—all within the lifetime of one of these trees."

"In geologic terms," I added, "merely a blink of an eye."

A sigh escaped Alexander. "It's tragic that the younger saplings here may not reach the longevity of these ancestral giants."

After carefully weighing our options, Alexander and I chose a spot in the valley's heart for our tent, undeterred by the peculiar sense of unease we both shared. Working in unison, we set up our camp in no time, ensuring our tent was securely staked, and a stockpile of firewood was within reach. All the while, despite no tangible threat, the eerie atmosphere lingered, keeping me on edge.

Over the course of the next few days, we painstakingly explored the vicinity. The stifling, humid heat posed a trial, yet our passion for adventure and discovery spurred us on. It felt as if we had combed every inch of the valley, yet our searches yielded no remarkable finds. By the fifth day, we conceded defeat. Any remnants that might have once existed within this fecund, pungent valley were likely reclaimed by the forest long ago. As I was engaged in disassembling our tent, contemplating this, Alexander's shout resonated from a short distance away.

"Abasi, you need to see this!"

"What is it?" I responded, my voice muted and echoless in the stifling forest humidity.

"I think I found something!"

Intrigued, I ambled over to him. "Found what exactly?"

We were standing at the base of one of the hills, where moss-laden boulders lay strewn about, likely remnants of a landslide from eons past.

"See that boulder leaning against the hillside? Look behind it," Alexander directed, his finger indicating a large rock. "Notice anything?"

A narrow crevice separated the boulder from the hill. It was so thin, I was amazed Alexander had even spotted it. Crouching, I tried to discern what was behind the boulder.

"Incredible..." I murmured to myself, realizing that the gap appeared to open up into a small cave entrance. "You think... could this possibly lead to a larger cave?"

"Only one way to find out," Alexander stated, a determined edge in his voice.

"I suppose," I said, my heart rate increasing. "But it could be a dead end." I tried to temper my enthusiasm. "Just a crack in the rock or a minor recess, maybe—"

"Enough guessing," Alexander interjected cheerfully, "Help me shift this rock. Let's not speculate about something we can easily investigate. After all, that's why we're here, isn't it?"

I offered no objections. With every ounce of our strength, we heaved the immense boulder aside. Once dislodged, it rolled onto some nearby bushes, flattening them under its weight. The entrance to the cave was not as shallow as I had feared, but it was claustrophobically narrow—a mere crawl space. Alexander crouched before it, cupped his hands to his mouth and bellowed:

"Hellooo!"

His voice echoed and dwindled, disappearing somewhere deep within the bedrock.

"We should probably think this through," I cautioned, "We could be stepping into unknown danger. Maybe we ought to report this to the authorities and let them handle it."

"And miss out on this adventure?" Alexander shook his head fervently. "We've been scouting for something like this for days. We can't just abandon it now."

"But we're stepping into the unknown," I protested. "There's no telling what awaits us inside that cave. We could get lost, or worse."

"We're equipped with helmets," Alexander said, already fastening his, "and we've explored tight spots before. We can manage."

"Those caves were charted, though," I said, "and they weren't *this* tight."

Alexander softened his tone, "We'll only venture far enough to get a sense of what lies within. No further."

I wavered, torn between caution and curiosity. Yet, the spark in Alexander's voice was infectious.

"Alright, fine," I said, "but we tread carefully. At the slightest sign of danger, we retreat. No arguments."

"Deal," Alexander affirmed, switching on his headlight.

The cave entrance was so narrow that had we been even marginally larger, we would never have fit. Although I wasn't claustrophobic, I couldn't say I had an affinity for such confined spaces; the mere thought of getting lodged in there sent chills down my spine. Hence, Alexander taking the lead was a welcome relief, as I followed close behind him. A few feet inside, we were met by an unexpected surge of cool, fresh air, drawn from the cave's hidden depths.

"Do you feel it?" Alexander asked as he pushed his body through the confined space. "That's a cross-breeze!"

"Great," I said, a weight lifting from my shoulders. "That means there's an opening up ahead. Let's keep going and see where it leads." With renewed determination, I pushed forward, eager to see what lay ahead.

The cool air emerging from the cave carried a fresh scent, serving as a much-needed relief after our day spent under the relentless heat. Soon, however, we began to freeze. I asked Alexander how the temperature could plummet so dramatically, beyond what could be accounted for by the airflow alone. Yet, he was just as mystified as I was.

"Is it getting tighter or wider?" I asked. "I can't tell."

"I'm not sure either," Alexander said.

We pressed on, undeterred by the mounting aches and pains coursing through our bodies. It was so narrow in some places that I thought I would have to break my ribs or dislocate an arm to get through. The cave ascended, forcing us to climb, before descending sharply and continuing, I believe, toward the south. The total absence of light except for the headlights on our helmets was suffocating. We eventually reached a pitch where we had to use our ropes to get down. We had never tried cave climbing before, and I felt stupid doing it now, given how risky it was. My fear was overwhelming, and my heart thudded wildly as we descended.

An unexpected slip sent my body reeling, swinging wildly on the rope. Panic took a stranglehold on me as I clung for dear life, the rough texture of the cave wall grating my skin with each successive bounce. My mind raced, desperately searching for a solution amid the disorienting spins. Just as I felt myself succumbing to the dread, a distant memory surfaced—advice given to me years ago about how to stabilize oneself when rappelling. I desperately reached for a nearby outcropping, the jagged rock grazing my fingers. After what seemed an agonizing stretch of time, I managed to grab hold, using the leverage to slow my wild swings. The friction against the rope, combined with the stabilizing force from the outcropping, gradually brought me to a halt.

"Are you okay?" Alexander's voice echoed from below. "I just reached the bottom."

"Thank God," I exhaled, relief washing over me. "Yeah, I think I'm okay."

Once I reached solid ground, we paused, allowing ourselves a moment to recuperate. If not for the tight confines that kept me in place, I would have been trembling. I knew we had already pushed our limits, but I couldn't bring myself to suggest retreat. Whether out of fear of being perceived as a quitter, or sheer enthrallment by the adventure, my silence was equally regrettable. Alexander, who was pressed up against me, proposed:

"Let's keep going. I think we're close to the exit."

Several more perilous squeezes ensued. The dust from the ground found its way into my mouth, making breathing an effort. I wasn't as hopeful as Alexander. In my view, this could drag on for hours, potentially culminating in a disastrous outcome. Before long, my concerns reached a boiling point, and I couldn't hold back from voicing my apprehensions.

"I'm thinking we should turn back," I started, struggling to keep my voice steady. "I'm feeling pretty worn out, and honestly, I'm starting to worry. We've been at this for more than an hour. Maybe we could try again tomorrow with some fresh energy?"

"Don't give up," Alexander replied. "Not to freak you out, but I'm not sure we can go back the way we came. It would be seriously rough, at least. There's no real place to turn around at the bottom of that pitch. Our best bet is to push forward and find the other opening. Besides, have you ever heard about that guy who tried to swim around the world but got tired halfway and swam back?"

The fear in his voice was clear even as he joked, something that scared me just as much as our predicament. We kept moving—slowly. I tried to focus on my breathing to calm myself down, but it didn't help. A few long, silent minutes later, Alexander spoke again:

"There's a gap ahead." His voice was firm, the fear seemingly gone. "It looks like it leads to a larger space. We're almost there."

After shoving Alexander through the narrow opening, he reciprocated by pulling me out as soon as he was free. We found ourselves in a chamber spacious enough for us to stand upright, the glare of our headlights our only source of illumination. Looking back at the minuscule hole we had emerged from, it was clear that we wouldn't be able to fit back through it. Squeezing oneself from such a confined space was one thing; willingly crawling back into it was quite another. This realization caused my heart to stutter in my chest. If the source of the cool air turned out to be equally impassable as the opening that brought us into this room, we would meet our end here.

I turned my headlight toward Alexander, illuminating his face. His frosty breaths, quick and shallow, revealed his fear was equal to my own. We swept our lights along the cave walls, and there it was—a second opening, seemingly just large enough to accommodate us. Relief was about to sweep over me when my eye caught something within the opening. Alexander saw it too. His voice echoed in the cavernous space, "My God, someone died here!"

It was a skeleton draped in a dark cloak. The lower half was obscured on the other side of the opening, suggesting they met their fate while struggling to crawl through.

"W-we might still have a chance," I stuttered, trembling. "This poor soul must have been larger than us, getting stuck in a hole of this size. So—" I halted, grappling with my emotions as the sight of the remains sent my pulse racing and my stomach churning. Regaining some composure, I picked up the thread, my voice gaining some steadiness, "What I'm saying is, if they made it this far before getting wedged in, we should be able to follow their route and find our way out."

We crouched beside the remains, examining them before daring to traverse the narrow passage where the person they belonged to had failed. The bones' coloration suggested they were anything but prehistoric. While devoid of any soft tissue, the skeleton still appeared relatively fresh. The skull lay face-down. Alexander carefully picked it up and held it under our gaze. Its empty sockets and bared teeth gave the illusion of a sinister grin.

"Put it away," I said. "It's giving me the creeps."

"Hold on," Alexander said. "Look at it. There's something—"

"What?"

"Don't you see it?"

In my heightened state of stress, nothing seemed amiss.

"Look at the elongation…" He rotated the skull. "The occipital region is massive, but the cranial vault is less rounded. See it?"

Though I could see what he pointed out, I struggled to grasp his inference. "So…?"

He swiveled the skull so its grinning visage faced us again. "The facial features are quite pronounced."

"What are you suggesting?"

"Heavy brow ridges, pronounced facial projection… Abasi, you might think I'm losing it, but I believe we're staring into the face of a Neanderthal."

"That's absurd," I retorted, despite the striking resemblance to the skulls from our studies. "The bones suggest this person died within the last hundred years."

"I'm aware," Alexander said, "yet, this skull bears all the hallmarks of a Neanderthal. Sure, Neanderthal DNA have been observed to influence human skull shapes, but this… this is too significant."

"Could the conditions in this cave have preserve the bones this well?" I asked.

"I can't say," Alexander admitted. "That would be astonishing too. Honestly, right now, I can't think of an explanation that wouldn't be."

Overwhelmed by a mélange of puzzlement, exhilaration, and

fear, we cautiously moved the remains from the opening so that we could leave, intent on reporting our unprecedented findings to the university. If our assumptions were correct, we had stumbled upon the most well-preserved Neanderthal skeleton in the world, a find of a lifetime. As I crawled inside the narrow passage, the prospect of etching our names in the annals of history consumed my thoughts.

The passages that lay ahead were just as arduous as the ones we'd already battled through. However, with the certainty of an eventual exit and the thrill of our discovery pushing us forward, our previous anxiety didn't return. I held some concern over how the paleontological community would perceive our amateurish venture, but I rationalized that our significant discovery would surely counterbalance our imprudence—at least to some extent. After what felt like an hour of continuous struggle, a welcome glint of light appeared at the cave's end, oddly doing nothing to alleviate the enduring chill.

"Something's not right," Alexander said as soon as I was out of the cave. "Look at the trees."

The leaves on the trees had undergone a dramatic transformation. No longer vibrant with shimmering shades of green, they were painted in strokes of sepia and amber. I blinked repeatedly, doubting the reliability of my own eyesight, the surreal shift in colors leaving me in a state of bewildered awe. The radiant heat of summer had changed as well; it had given way to a damp, earthy scent of wet soil and decomposing leaves. And above, hidden behind the fiery canopy, the sun was dimmed by a dreary overcast.

Alexander gaped at the transformed landscape, his face pale. "How is this possible?" A tense smile twitched at the corners of his mouth. "It's only August, and we were inside that cave for mere hours."

I peered around us, spotting more anomalies. "Look at the hills," I said, indicating their familiar contours. "We're still in the valley."

"Not just that." Alexander nodded toward the cave. "This is where we entered. I mean…" He paused briefly, as if unsure of how to proceed. "This is the same opening. Although, it's different somehow. That boulder was to the right before, wasn't it?"

"Did we circle back without realizing?" I asked.

"Perhaps," Alexander said, "but there's clearly more at play here. Just how long were we in that cave?"

"The sun's position is right for August.," I said, glancing at my watch. "It's the same day, just not the same climate."

"But how?" Alexander said. "It doesn't make any sense."

"That's an understatement," I said. "Let's get back to camp and see what condition it's in."

We battled our way through near-impenetrable thickets, searching fervently for any sign of our tent. But, to our disbelief, it was gone.

"Are you sure this is where we set it up?" Alexander asked. "It must be, right?"

"This feels wrong," I said. "It's like the world's been tilted on its axis, and not just figuratively. I think we should try and go back… try to squeeze—"

Ignoring me, Alexander pulled out his phone. "No reception," he announced, already heading for the hillside. "We should climb and get a better view."

I hesitated, a sense of dread curling in my gut. "Alexander, wait, I have a bad—"

He cut me off. "We need to understand what's happening!"

I remained on the ground, watching him start up the slope,

and couldn't help but think about how fearless he always seemed. It was one of the things I admired about him, but in this situation, it also made me worry. I couldn't shake the feeling that we were in over our heads.

"Don't just stand there!" Alexander yelled. "Get moving!"

Taking a deep breath and closing my eyes as though invoking divine help, I managed to shake off my paralysis. Upon reaching the hill's summit, the Białowieża Forest sprawled before us. Its once lush canopy had transformed into a scarlet sea, its tranquillity disturbed by maroon waves led by the wind among the leaves. From the melancholy sky, a soft rain began to fall. I spun around, desperately seeking a familiar landmark to anchor my disoriented senses. But nothing came to my aid. Dizziness overwhelmed me. I halted, staring down at my feet before pressing my hands to my forehead as if to still the spinning sensation. "This-this is insane," I stammered. "It's utterly... inexplicable."

Alexander placed a reassuring hand on my shoulder. "Take it easy," he said, "you're having an anxiety attack."

I became acutely aware of my ragged, rapid breaths and forced myself to slow them, to fill my lungs and then exhale fully. As I began to regain some semblance of control, my new-found calm was shattered by a gunshot cracking through the stillness of the forest below. Two more shots echoed, a disturbing staccato, before silence returned.

"People," Alexander noted. "Let's make our way down and see who they are. Perhaps they can shed light on what's happening."

"But they're armed," I said. "It's dangerous."

"We'll tread carefully," he reassured me. "Look at it this way, what other choice do we have? Going back through the cave isn't feasible; squeezing through that narrow passage again seems impossible. We're effectively trapped here, so it's imperative we figure out where 'here' is."

I hesitated, but Alexander had already started descending.

"Aren't you curious?" He glanced back at me. "We've stumbled upon a phenomenon that defies current scientific understanding. As explorers, isn't it our obligation to gather as much information as we can about this... this anomaly? It's more than just an abrupt climatic change."

"I'm starting to think that we're still inside the cave," I quipped half-heartedly as I followed Alexander, "hallucinating this while succumbing to carbon dioxide poisoning."

As we navigated the rocky slope, the valley's silence gradually gave way to the full symphony of the forest. Unrecognizable birdsong echoed from the treetops, streams burbled down the hill, winds whispered through the forest floor, and faint barking resonated in the distance. By the time we reached the bottom, the forest's cacophony had fully returned.

"Let's track down those dogs," Alexander said. "They might belong to the people. I wouldn't be surprised if they're part of a hunting party."

Sneaking through the dense vegetation, doing our best to stay quiet, we began hearing indiscernible voices a few hundred feet ahead. Alexander crouched down and told me to do the same, and then we crawled through yellowed ferns until we reached a fallen tree that was big enough to hide behind. From there, the voices became clear albeit still impossible to understand. The group spoke a language we had never heard before. It echoed the rhythmic patterns of Khoisan, but instead of the characteristic clicks, deep knocking sounds resonated from the depths of their throats. Despite my head-shaking plea for caution, Alexander's curiosity proved too strong to resist. He carefully lifted his head to sneak a peek, then hastily lowered it back to safety. His eyes were wide with excitement as he silently formed a single word, "Mammoth!"

I stared at him, perplexed. He nodded as if to encourage me to look for myself. I hesitated at first, but ultimately succumbed to my curiosity. A dead animal covered in thick fur lay on the ground, partly shrouded in a crawling mist. The enormous tusks removed all doubts: it *was* a mammoth. Five figures swathed in black cloaks encircled the carcass, each clutching what looked like large double-barreled shotguns. Wisps of smoke drifted lazily into the air from large cigars held by two of them. Their faces remained concealed, hidden under the shadowy depths of their hoods, yet their attire resonated an eerie similarity with the individual we had discovered in the cave. In shock, I mouthed, "Neanderthals."

One of them lifted what appeared to be a whistle to their lips, yet no audible sound filled the air—at least, none we could discern. Within moments, four hulking creatures lumbered from the surrounding woods, joining the cloaked figures. Their size mirrored that of grizzly bears, yet their faces bore a wolfish semblance. My initial thought was that they were predators, drawn to the mammoth carcass. But when one of them let out a bark, a cold realization washed over me. These were not wild beasts, but the very dogs whose distant calls we had heard earlier.

We slid back down, pressing our backs against the rough bark of the trunk. I swallowed hard, forcing a shaky whisper, "It's like... like we've journeyed back to the Middle Paleolithic!"

Alexander raised an eyebrow at me. "Do you seriously believe Neanderthals possessed rifles in those times? As you pointed out, this is the same day. It's just not the same Earth."

"Wha-what do you mean?" I stammered.

"Simply this: our gun-toting friends over there," he subtly nodded toward the cloaked figures, "are evidence that Neanderthals didn't go extinct in this world, wherever it is."

"That's preposterous, I don't believe—" A guttural growl resonated behind us, cutting me short.

Alexander's grip tightened on my arm. "You better believe it!"

The beast charged at us. We had no choice but to get up and run—right into the arms of the cloaked figures.

The figures closed in around us, their rifles aimed at our chests. They were imposing—not taller, but much more robust than an average man, or rather, an anatomically modern human. Despite their deep, resonating knocks and indecipherable words defying our understanding, their gestures clearly conveyed that their distress mirrored our own. As they drew closer, the shadows cast by their hoods lessened, revealing their distinctly Neanderthal features more clearly.

"What are they going to do?" I asked more to myself than anyone else.

One of the Neanderthals barked a command, "Halufska!"

Almost instinctively, we dropped to our knees, hands raised above our heads. I closed my eyes, whispering silent pleas for mercy. The ragged breath of one of their dogs pricked at the nape of my neck, its sporadic growls threatening an imminent attack. The sensation sent chills down my spine, somehow striking more terror into my heart than the menacing rifles.

Beside me, Alexander battled his own fear, attempting to establish communication. He pointed at himself slowly, stating his name with a shaky steadiness. Encouraged by his actions, I dared to crack my eyes open. The Neanderthal who had shouted at us was now crouched down, scrutinizing Alexander. After a moment of silence, he grunted something unintelligible, seemingly a comment directed to his comrades rather than a self-introduction.

He then swung his weather-beaten face my way. His hand

extended, touching my face with the caution of someone approaching an open flame. I recoiled instinctively, and he yanked his hand back in surprise. As I looked back at him, a rush of terror surging through my veins, my eyes were drawn to his teeth. They were startlingly white and impeccably cared for—an odd touch of modernity, even more profound than the rifles they wielded.

"Alex," my friend repeated, his palm pressed firmly against his chest.

Still ignoring his attempts at communication, the Neanderthal stood tall, taking a moment to light his cigar with a chunky, elongated match.

"I don't want to die," I murmured, my gaze flickering to my friend. "I told you we should have—"

"Stay calm," Alexander interjected quickly, the urgency in his tone betraying his attempt to reassure himself as much as me. "If they had wanted to kill us, they would have done it by now."

Following a brief exchange amongst themselves, one of them knelt behind us. Roughly, he bound our hands behind our backs, the coarse fibers biting into my skin as he cinched the rope tight around my wrists. I had to bite back a wince, striving to remain still. The Neanderthal that had approached us first, who I had perceived as the leader, left the area with one of the dogs. Returning a short while later with urgency etched on his face, he gestured to his companions, who quickly pulled us to our feet and led us away. Moving into the forest, they left behind their freshly killed animal—a promising sign that we held some value to them. Yet, the pivotal question following that conclusion—*for what purpose?*—kept the terror firmly in place.

After a considerable trek, we found ourselves standing before a dirt road.

"Jesus Christ!" Alexander blurted out. "They've invented motor vehicles!"

Indeed, a formidable, black behemoth of a vehicle loomed before us. With eight wheels—six in the rear and two up front—it bore a closer resemblance to a diesel locomotive than a conventional truck. One of the hunters swung open the back doors, revealing a cargo hold reeking of raw meat and gasoline. The lead hunter ushered us inside, pushing us toward a bench affixed to the wall. Two of them followed and took a seat opposite us, their watchful eyes scrutinizing our every move in silence. Their rugged faces were barely visible, faintly lit by the meager glow filtering through two small windows on the back doors. They both lit cigars, the flickering flames casting eerie shadows onto their stone-carved features. With a shuddering rumble and a series of pops from the engine, the vehicle lurched into motion. We sat in tense silence, wary of provoking our captors. Only when their focus drifted toward their own conversation—undoubtedly about us—did Alexander dare to lean in and whisper:

"I wonder what happened to our species in this world."

"Anything could have," I replied, struggling to push down my rising panic. "History is fragile, you need to change very little to change everything."

"So, you're saying someone stepped on a butterfly in this world but not in ours?" Alexander said. "It depends on the timing, I suppose. The further back in time the deviation, the smaller it could be. Imagine that, a particle moving left instead of right and poof—"

"What do you think they'll do to us?" I said, lethal fear derailing my ability to follow his abstract musings. "Do you think they'll kill us?"

One of the Neanderthals looked straight at me, forcing me to divert my eyes.

"The key lies in the answer to my question—what happened to *Homo sapiens* in this world? If they see our species as mortal enemies, we might very well be doomed, but if we died out thousands of years ago, they'll probably want to keep us alive for scientific reasons."

As the fading sunlight was our only connection to the world outside, we relied on the jolts and bumps of our journey to paint a picture of our surroundings. As the truck barreled ahead, the road's roughness diminished, suggesting we had transitioned onto their version of a highway. But the familiar sounds of passing vehicles were eerily absent—leading me to surmise that traffic here didn't exist in the way I was accustomed to back home.

"They're remarkably similar to us," I said, my fear now abated enough to allow for contemplation. "I'm not surprised they domesticated the dog, even though they bred them into something entirely different than us, but I would never have guessed they could reach the industrial age."

"And yet they're also remarkably different from us," Alexander pointed out. "For instance, they didn't wipe out the European megafauna."

"That's true," I said. "And that points to a smaller population, just like we suspected."

"Which in turn could explain the early autumn," Alexander said. "A sparser population of hominids over forty thousand years would have meant fewer carbon dioxide emissions, resulting in a cooler climate with less of the season creep we've observed back home."

"What level of technology do you reckon they're at?" I asked. "Their rifles are quite rudimentary—iron sights, no scopes. They don't strike me as particularly modern. The vehicle, on the other hand, appears a touch more advanced."

"Don't forget their larger eyes and areas of the brain devoted to vision," Alexander said. "Maybe they don't need scopes because of their superior sight. Also, technology doesn't necessarily develop along the same path in all societies. In either case, it's clear that they have mastered the art of science and engineering. That in itself is astonishing."

My anxiety flared anew as the vehicle ground to a halt, the uncertainty of what awaited us outside looming large.

One of the hunters cranked the doors open, flooding the truck with a feeble light. As we stepped out, we found ourselves engulfed by the enormity of an underground garage that echoed the brutalist architecture I had encountered in Prague a few years earlier. The unpainted concrete surrounding us bore a peculiar shade of blue, dimly lit by large spherical lamps of white glass suspended from the lofty ceiling.

A handful of vehicles sat parked against the walls, none resembling the truck that brought us. They were smaller, akin to regular cars, and uniformly dark and indistinguishable in the dim light. Amidst them, the hunters' truck was a distinct outlier, suggesting this was not its usual destination. One of the hunters picked up a dashboard radio, interrupting the silence with a crackle of static. Moments later, the piercing creak of a small metal door echoed through the monolithic space, drawing startled looks from us and the hunters alike. Those smoking snuffed out their cigars with haste as if fearing they might be caught with them.

Three shadows emerged from the yawning doorway. The hunting party straightened, prodding us to follow suit. Clad in garments of finer fabric than the hunters' cloaks, the figures hid their faces behind veils, allowing only their eyes to peer through. Moving with a graceful authority, their presence induced a palpable silence among us, broken only by the uneven, nervous breaths of our captors. As they neared, it became clear that they were women.

As soon as they got a closer look at us, their eyes lit up with unmistakable fascination. I guessed they hadn't fully understood, or perhaps believed, what the hunters had radioed in. One of them retrieved what resembled a walkie-talkie, speaking into it without taking her eyes off us. The woman next to her unclipped a baton from her belt and tapped my helmet as if to check if it was real. We must have seemed utterly alien to them, our oddity magnified not only by our distinct anatomy but also by our colorful caving gear.

One of the women ushered the hunters through a separate door, likely for debriefing, while the remaining pair guided Alexander and me toward the door they had entered from. Behind it, a small platform nestled within a vertical shaft greeted us. Upon stepping onto it, one of the women hauled a lever, causing the platform to ascend with a steady metallic clatter—revealing it to be an elevator of sorts, bereft of an enclosed cabin and accompanied by intermittent electrical hums from its edges. My clothes brushed against the rough concrete, but I held still, preferring the abrasive touch to standing too close to our escorts. Glancing upward, the height of the structure became apparent—it was a towering edifice, potentially five hundred feet tall or more. Our ascent halted after just a few levels, at which point we were led into a compact room where they freed our hands and directed us to sit in a pair of sturdy chairs.

Outside the room, activity surged. Women—seemingly no men—darted back and forth, engaged in hurried conversations or issuing rapid-fire instructions through their walkie-talkies. It was clear they hadn't anticipated our arrival. A steady stream of these uniformed women came and went, some attempting dialogue, others merely observing with curiosity. We spent what felt like an eternity in this small room, hostages to their indecision. A gnawing need for the bathroom began to plague me, but I was at a loss for how to communicate it. The stalemate was finally broken when one of the earlier women reappeared, sharply tapping our chairs with her baton and issuing a stern command. It seemed our stay in this room had come to an end at last.

"Aside from being ordered around like this," Alexander noted, glancing around as we were led through a corridor brimming with curious eyes, "they aren't particularly hostile."

"I don't know," I said. "They aren't exactly friendly either."

Flanked by two male guards armed with pistol-like weapons, we were led through a doorway into a room that bore the resemblance of a hastily cleared locker room, its walls and floor a grid of grey tiles. Our belongings were swiftly seized. Handing over my helmet to the woman who had earlier tapped on it, I activated the headlight, demonstrating its function. Their reactions, somewhat blasé, suggested they were familiar with similar devices. The vibrant plastic of our equipment intrigued them far more, leading me to suspect that they had yet to discover or make use of hard plastic. Based on this assumption, I speculated they might be trailing our own world by a half-century or more in technological advancements.

"Plastic," Alexander said, knocking on his own helmet, without being understood.

Our clothes were swiftly removed, and we were gestured toward several showers. Covering our privates with our hands, we awkwardly positioned ourselves beneath them, feeling acutely exposed before the watchful eyes of our captors. The showers offered no sanctuary or privacy—they were nothing more than stark fixtures lined up in the center of the monochrome room. A guard twisted a knob, and a blast of icy water erupted from the showerheads. It was bracingly cold, but probably not intentionally so. Given their acclimation to frigid conditions, this might have been how they preferred to shower themselves.

After our chilling rinse, they provided us with a pair of yellow overalls. Ill-fitting though they were, they brought a welcome layer of warmth.

"Finally, some color," Alexander remarked, attempting to summon a smile to his frost-nipped face. "I was beginning to think color was outlawed here."

We were escorted down a grand hallway, lined by towering doors. Many were slightly ajar, revealing clusters of curious women hiding their faces behind identical veils, their attention focused on us as we passed by.

"Their culture appears uniform and simplistic," Alexander continued in a whisper. "Although I don't think it's simple by any means... It's rational."

"And pompous," I added. "Just look at this hallway. These doors would fit a mammoth!"

"Minimalistic yet bombastic." Alexander looked up at the high ceiling. "I wonder what it says about them as a people."

The male guards led us to a nondescript door in the middle of the corridor, leading to a room akin to a high school chemistry lab with rows of metal tables and walls adorned with unrecognizable scientific equipment. We were steered to a desk at the other end of the room, where three women waited, their faces obscured by yellow protective masks rather than the ubiquitous dark veils. Some of our belongings, including our phones, lay neatly arrayed on the desk. The woman in the center gestured toward them, clearly asking for a demonstration. I hesitated, unsure if showing them was a good idea, but Alexander was quick to act, promptly unlocking his phone.

"Wait," I cautioned, "Should we really—"

"Relax," Alexander said. "Showing them our technology could make us more valuable to them."

His logic was sound, yet my instincts rebelled. Biting back my misgivings, I watched as he navigated through various apps on his phone. The women leaned in, utterly captivated. The lack of an internet connection, rendering most apps useless, didn't diminish their fascination. Even the male guards, seemingly limited to strictly defined duties, found themselves drawn to the spectacle. Alexander reveled in the attention, a proud smile brightening his face. Filled with the same unease since we left the valley, I recoiled at his confidence. To me, it all seemed eerily off somehow—not just this dark realm, but our arrival to it as well. It was an inkling, an unverifiable suspicion, yet it felt as if every step henceforth would be an affront to nature herself.

Alexander pulled up his gallery and played a video for the Neanderthals, footage captured during a climate change protest in New York. This offered their first sight of our world. Their initial fascination morphed into a discernible concern as they watched the shimmering skyscrapers enveloping Times Square and countless protesters, chaotic and determined, flooding the streets with their defiant cries.

"America," Alexander clarified, gesturing toward the screen.

Once the video ended, the women regarded us with a disquieting suspicion. They exchanged a brief, hushed dialogue among themselves before one reached for a mouthpiece attached to the wall, pressing one of its few buttons—apparently placing a call. Their conversation eluded me, but the serious tone didn't.

After a moment of internal discussion among the women, they guided us back toward the elevator, with the armed guards trailing closely. This time, we ascended to the topmost floor. The corridors here mirrored those we'd seen below, albeit less crowded. At the end of the hallway, a grand door hinted at an area of special importance beyond. Adjacent to the door, white symbols, inscribed in a curvaceous, lavish script, provided an unexpected touch of elegance amidst the building's otherwise stark aesthetic.

One of the women pressed a small metallic button centered on the door. Despite the absence of sound, it seemed to function as a doorbell. As we awaited entry, the distant blare of an alarm—reminiscent of a mechanical foghorn—resounded from outside. The building responded with a subtle tremor, shaking loose a shower of dust from the ceiling. I exchanged a glance with Alexander, but our Neanderthal hosts appeared unperturbed by the alarm.

As the door slid open automatically, we were ushered inside. The male guards held their posts at the entrance, leaving us in the expansive domain of what was unmistakably a high-ranking office. A lavish black carpet, fashioned from some animal's skin, stretched across much of the floor, leading to a formidable desk. Seated behind it was a middle-aged woman ensconced in a chair with an exaggeratedly high backrest. In contrast to the others, her face was bare. Fiery, long curls framed her face, and her eyes, rheumy and ice-blue, analyzed us. Clad in a garment reminiscent of a jumpsuit, she took a draw from an oddly shaped pipe, releasing a blend of tobacco and marijuana. Behind her, a large window stood out against the otherwise solid wall, our first sight of one so far. It revealed only darkness, indicating we weren't in a city. Perhaps, I thought, they didn't even have cities.

The veiled women positioned their batons at the backs of our knees, a silent directive to kneel before the weighty desk. I complied instantly, but Alexander hesitated, attempting to put on a brave face. A swift strike to his thigh had him joining me on the floor, grimacing as he battled his discomfort.

"Just do as they ask," I implored him. "Don't provoke them."

"We can't appear weak," he managed through gritted teeth, his voice strained by pain. "If they value strength, any signs of weakness might encourage them to treat us more harshly."

"That's a dangerous guess," I said. "They appear much more devoted to respect for hierarchy and knowing one's place."

The woman behind the desk studied us with an appraising gaze, as though deciphering a complex puzzle. Eventually, she rose from her chair, striding toward us, prompting a tremor of fear to ripple through my body. As the women conversed overhead, Alexander asserted:

"They won't hurt us, we hold too much value for them."

"But that doesn't mean freedom," I retorted. "I don't want to end up a specimen in their lab. They might not kill us, but they won't just let us leave."

"We'll figure out a way—" Alexander started, only to be cut off by the jumpsuit-clad woman.

She signaled for us to rise, her gesture clear despite the language barrier. Without hesitation, Alexander complied, keen to avoid repeating his earlier misstep, while I remained frozen in place, immobilized by shock. One of the women took hold of my arm and deftly hoisted me to my feet. The older woman, who clearly wielded authority here, addressed us, but her words were lost in translation—although by context, it might have been a question.

Positioning herself beside a monochromatic world map hung between two towering wooden shelves brimming with bind-bound books, she motioned for us to approach. Weeding through our hesitation, we complied. At first, the map didn't match my understanding of Earth. Spurred by curiosity, Alexander ventured forward. Encouraged by his boldness and the woman's receptive demeanor, I followed tentatively.

"I don't understand," I confessed, fixating on the map. "What kind of—"

The woman spoke again, her tone more assertive. She seemed to want us to pinpoint our origin on the map. Alexander promptly responded, placing his finger on a location.

"This is Africa," he declared.

It was only when he pointed it out that I noticed the peculiarities of the map. Unlike the north-up maps at home, this one was oriented south-up, slightly skewed to place central Europe in the middle, and presented the relative sizes of the landmasses in an unconventional manner.

Unable to illustrate our exact point of origin with any hope of comprehension, Alexander attempted to convey the birthplace of our species instead. He resorted to an array of vague gestures, miming the distant past—an attempt that garnered little more than a blend of confusion and skepticism from the woman.

"Look," Alexander said, pointing at the map again. "The Sahara—it's so much smaller here."

The woman scrutinized us intently as we examined the map, indifferent puffs of smoke occasionally clouding our vision. I frequently found myself stealing anxious glances at her before voicing my thoughts, seeking some tacit permission to speak.

"These pictograms," I said, pointing at silhouettes of black skulls dispersed across the map, each encircled by dotted lines of varying sizes, "could they represent some sort of dead zones?"

Alexander offered a different perspective. "You're still viewing the map through the lens of our own culture," he said. "I don't think they symbolize death here, but rather *themselves*. They could be cities or even city-states."

"They don't seem to have conventional countries," I noted,

my finger tracing a solitary border stretching from the Ural Mountains down to Australia. A bold red line, the only splash of color on the map, demarcated Europe from Asia. "What do you suppose is the significance of—"

Alexander interrupted, his finger hovering over the region analogous to Russia in our world, slowly migrating southward. "The skull symbols differ on the other side of the boundary, do you see that?"

"Could it be...?" I started, grappling with the implications of his discovery. "Are you suggesting—"

"Denisovans!" Alexander burst out so abruptly that the two women behind us instinctively reached for their batons. Lowering his voice, he continued, "It actually makes sense. If Neanderthals had a smaller population, they might not have driven the Denisovans to extinction. This is beyond incredible, Abasi." His fear was now eclipsed by sheer fascination. "This world isn't ruled by a single hominid species, but by two."

The Neanderthal skulls were strewn across Europe, Africa, and the majority of the New World, while Denisovan skulls marked Asia and portions of western North America. Predictably, the polar ice caps were more expansive in this world, but that hadn't deterred the Neanderthals from inhabiting regions near the North Pole, including settlements in Greenland. Despite these two species' global dispersion, the total number of population centers—if that was indeed what the skulls represented—was markedly fewer than the number of cities in most countries in our world.

The woman, seemingly satiated by our examination of the map, retreated back to her desk. She picked up a mouthpiece and began a brisk, vehement conversation with an unseen recipient on the other end of the line. The alarm we had heard earlier blared again, the sound amplified by our proximity to the window. Unfazed by the disturbance, the woman merely elevated her voice to rise above the clamor. A flicker of electric lights cut through the darkness outside, but they did little to illuminate the scene. Not a minute later, a blazing explosion erupted several miles away, its aftershock sending tremors through our building.

"Dear God," Alexander gasped, "It's a rocket!"

The rocket's body was swallowed by the obsidian night, yet the trail of fire beneath it signaled a powerful ascent.

"The real question," I added, watching the spectacle, "is whether it's bound for space or aimed at the Denisovans."

Following the enigmatic meeting with the woman, we were promptly escorted away by the other women. They led us to the elevator, initiating our descent with a downward pull of the lever. The platform plunged so quickly that the acceleration sent a jolt through my chest. We whizzed past successive floors, breezed through the garage, and then there was nothing but the encircling concrete walls. Still, our descent continued unabated. My anxiety spiked, exacerbating the perspiration soaking my thick, yellow overalls. An acrid smell became more and more apparent the farther down we went. One of the women glanced at me, muttered something indecipherable, then coaxed me toward the platform's center. Moments later, the wall nearest to me yielded to an expansive vista of a vast cave, faintly illuminated by countless twinkling specks of light that stippled the precipitous cliffs and profound chasms. Hundreds of individuals, reduced to minute shadows against the dim bedrock, traversed the expansive underground quarry with solemn grace, accentuated by the intermittent grazing of the terrain by the headlights of trucks shuttling to and fro. My suffocating sense of engulfment on the descending platform instantly turned into dizzying vertigo.

Our descent concluded after several disorienting minutes. We were greeted by two male guards swathed in cloaks. After conferring with them, the women left us in their charge and ascended back to the surface. As they herded us through the darkness, it became chillingly evident that we were at the base of a mine functioning also as a subterranean labor camp. The rough-hewn bedrock was punctuated with cells, each barred and housing four to five inmates dressed in yellow overalls mirroring our own—a sight that dropped my heart into a pit of dread.

"Denisovans," Alexander murmured, gesturing toward the captives. "Our predictions about their appearance were fairly accurate, it seems."

Indeed, most of the prisoners weren't Neanderthals. While there was a resemblance—certainly more than with us—distinctive attributes set them apart. As Alexander implied, these remarkably aligned with the descriptions suggested by the epigenetic analyses conducted back home. Their skin bore a darker hue, their wide, almond-shaped eyes a deep brown, and their hands—grasping the prison bars as they watched us pass—were more slender and delicate than their Neanderthal counterparts.

The darkness was suffocating, barely punctured by the dim glow of small lamps suspended from the ceiling by thick cables. The air was heavy with a noxious mix of rock dust, sulfur dioxide, burnt coal, tobacco, and the unmistakable scent of excrement. Prisoners moving in weary columns, burdened by the shovels, pickaxes, hammers, chisels, and pans they carried, marched relentlessly into the depths of the mine under the stern command and occasional whip lashings from cloaked Neanderthal overseers.

"Think they're done with us?" I found myself asking. "Will we end up here, too?"

"They've seen the evidence," Alexander replied, his tone distant. "They know our world exists. They might either discard us in their attempts to reach it or solicit our assistance. It's hard to say."

Our conversation was cut short when they herded us into an unoccupied cell overlooking the mine. Two beds, mere slabs of hardness, hung from chains on the damp stone wall, forming a frameless bunk. A metal bucket served as our toilet and overwhelmed by necessity, we made use of it immediately—filling the confines with a lingering stench. Overcome by exhaustion, I then collapsed on the lower bunk. I buried my face in my palms, too weary to think. All I could do was surrender to the symphony of clinking pickaxes, cracking whips, and the agonized screams of Denisovans echoing in my ears.

"Poor beings," I said.

"There's probably a similar mine back in Asia, teeming with Neanderthals," Alexander said, his gaze lost in the view outside the bars. "There's a certain balance here, you know."

"What do you mean?" I asked.

"Everyone has their corner of the world," he said. "The animals aren't being systematically hunted to extinction, and the environment isn't collapsing under relentless exploitation. It just took a few *Homo sapiens* escaping Africa to ruin all of it. We spread like a raging wildfire."

"You've certainly got a knack for finding a silver lining," I retorted, a hollow smile playing on my lips. "How do we get out of this mess, anyway?"

"I don't know," he said. "Our situation may seem bleak, but a change in perspective could help. Don't consider yourself a prisoner, Abasi, but a primatologist doing fieldwork. In essence, isn't this similar to what other researchers have willingly subjected themselves to in hostile environments? Just think of Jane Goodall, or better yet, Richard and Meave Leakey—"

"But we *are* prisoners," I said. "It's hard to perceive it differently while confined behind these bars."

Alexander didn't respond, his thoughts seemingly far away. The uncompromising firmness of the stained mattress pressed against me, its stark austerity heightened by the absence of bedclothes or pillows, but despite the discomfort, sleep claimed me the moment my eyes closed. An image of my mother surfaced in my mind, steadily gaining in clarity until I found myself in the kitchen of our old home, watching her laugh and spin tales for my two younger sisters as she prepared dinner. A pang of sorrow struck me, abruptly bringing me back to reality with the echoing sound of Alexander's voice within our confined space:

"Their matriarchal structures are interesting, don't you think? Considering their apparent lack of gender-based specialization, a central premise in my doctoral thesis, I would have envisioned a society less steeped in patriarchy, perhaps even leaning toward egalitarianism. But an elitist matriarchy? That's quite the curveball."

"I'm not sure it's that surprising," I replied, trying to shake off the lingering sadness from my dream. "If their gender roles are a relatively recent development, ideas might have played a larger role in shaping them than genes." Pondering further, I added, "Perhaps they didn't have the same social hierarchies as us, leading to the females never evolving a sexual attraction to dominance and hence driving the males to physical labor instead of political power. I mean, if they didn't have any pack leaders, maybe females selected males solely based on physical abilities."

Alexander responded with a forced chuckle, "So you're suggesting Neanderthal males had no reproductive incentives to gain social status and left all the tedious administrative tasks to the females, while they were out enjoying time with their mates? Classic."

"I don't know," I said. "I'm merely speculating here, it's all conjecture, really. So please, don't quote me in your thesis." The last words were barely out before I succumbed to sleep again.

I awoke a few hours later, jolted out of slumber by a guard depositing a metallic tray laden with food and water. The food—gray porridge served in coarse wooden bowls—bore a striking resemblance to gruel. Its only semblance to a balanced diet was a smattering of larvae, whether added intentionally or the result of neglect, I couldn't tell. The ordeal of swallowing it without retching was only slightly mitigated by the accompaniment of a dry, pallid slice of bread.

Our days blended into a monotony of confinement, each punctuated by the morning visit of another prisoner—a Neanderthal afflicted with dwarfism who came to empty our waste bucket. At first, he was clearly afraid of us. But with each successive encounter, emboldened by our attempts to communicate and show sympathy, he slowly inched closer. I was on the verge of offering him bread and my name when the woman in the jumpsuit arrived, flanked by a phalanx of armed guards. With a threatening wave of her baton, she scared off our newfound acquaintance.

"Hey, he didn't do anything!" Alexander protested.

Ignoring his outcry, the woman ordered one of the guards to unlock the cell. Held in a hushed dread, too terrified to utter a word, we were herded through the labyrinthine mine, scrutinized by an array of soot-streaked faces lurking in the obscurity. We were pushed onto an ascending platform, and as it rose, my emotions tangled into a knot of relief at our escape from the subterranean gloom and anxiety about what awaited us above. Our captors set a swift pace, and any hint of lagging due to fatigue was met with a sharp prod to quicken our steps. I kept my gaze low, fearing direct confrontation with our guards, tracking the synchronized march of the Neanderthals' feet through corridors awash in shades of Prussian blue. Our journey was halted abruptly, nearly sending me sprawling forward. A pair of formidable metal doors stood imposingly before us. With a resonating groan, two guards cranked them open, unleashing a blaze of daylight that seared my eyes. Shading them with a raised arm, we were brought outside, where I soon realized that the perceived brightness was merely the dull light of a gloomy afternoon. Taking a deep breath, I relished the fresh air with its hint of impending rain, feeling a surge of vitality that allowed me to venture a look around.

Standing on an expansive square hemmed in by towering, featureless columns, I was awestruck by the monolithic structure from which we'd been ushered. It was a stunning contrast to our dismal surroundings—a stark tower of white marble that exuded an aura of antiquity amidst the bleakness.

In the square's center, a battalion of about fifty Neanderthal men stood in a rigid formation, overseen by a female commander energetically addressing them. Dressed in high-collared, charcoal-colored jackets, steel helmets, and sturdy boots, these men radiated an unnerving authority. Their gloved hands cradled rifles equipped with bayonets, and machete-like blades swung from their belts.

"Soldiers," I muttered. "This is either our execution ground or—"

"My God!" Alexander interrupted, pointing skyward. "Look at that!"

Through the lingering mist, accompanied by the resonant call of a nearby horn, a behemoth of an airship loomed into view, its dark silhouette akin to a menacing zeppelin. Soldiers scattered to grab the lines thrown from the ship, aiding its landing. The remaining soldiers formed an honor guard flanking the ship's entrance, their commander positioning herself at the forefront, ready to receive the incoming guests. We were maneuvered forward until we stood behind her. Veiled women streamed out of the tower behind us, positioning themselves in our rear. It was clear that this grand spectacle had been orchestrated for us—or rather, for the benefit of the higher-ups aboard the airship who were undoubtedly here to conduct their own examination of us.

As the doors swung open, we watched in anticipation. Another group of women appeared, adorned in crimson uniforms unlike anything we'd seen before. With purposeful strides, they advanced toward us. The commander standing before us acknowledged their arrival with a respectful salute, tilting her head gracefully to the right. This gesture was echoed by the rest of the onlookers, and, caught in the moment, I found myself following suit, though my bow was not as practiced as theirs. Each member of the group in red subjected us to a close examination. Notably, an elderly woman, distinguished by her gray hair, scrutinized me in detail, taking hold of my chin and methodically shifting my face from side to side—ignoring the terror in my eyes.

As the women sternly addressed the reception party before transitioning into more subdued discussions among themselves, fear seized me. Being out of the dank cell was a welcome change, but I was under no illusions—I was still captive and likely to remain so indefinitely. Thoughts of escape seemed like delusions of the desperate. My mind wandered to my parents, who had planned to visit me in Paris later that summer. The image of them standing in my dormitory, sifting through my belongings in search of some hint of my disappearance, was gut-wrenching.

The agonizing thought of them forever questioning my fate, perpetually deprived of closure, weighed heavily on me.

Our situation's gravity was further emphasized when additional soldiers disembarked from the airship, bolstering the security personnel on-site. A bus-like vehicle rumbled toward us from an arched opening across the square, churning up an ashen cloud that hovered in the cold air.

We climbed aboard alongside the crimson-uniformed women and a handful of soldiers. The inside mirrored that of a subway car, with benches lining the walls. Alexander and I were nudged to the back while the others occupied the middle, their voices straining against the thrumming engine. As we moved, I peered out at the dreary buildings encircling the white tower, their desolation accentuated by the sight of a blue-gray rocket being trundled toward the launchpad.

Alexander leaned in close. "It resembles a V2," he whispered. "Likely a missile."

"Any guess on the payload?" I asked.

"I doubt it's designed for mass destruction," Alexander responded. "Considering the lack of large population centers here, there wouldn't be a need for high-yield bombs. These missiles, if that's what they are, likely serve more as instruments of terror than tools of mass murder."

"That's camouflage," I observed, pointing at the blue hue on the missile's underside. "It's designed to blend in with the sky when airborne. This suggests two things: one, it's indeed a missile; and two, their adversaries have the capability to intercept it. If their enemies are the Denisovans, they must possess similar technological prowess."

Alexander nodded, "Their warfare must look vastly different from ours. Just imagine it. They've likely never had to deal with an army exceeding ten thousand soldiers, given their smaller populations. They've never had their equivalent of the Battle of the Somme. Look at their weaponry. They aren't automatic. It's unlikely they've ever had to mow down thousands of enemy troops with machine guns."

"Automatic rifles weren't necessarily created for mass killings," I countered, "but more for providing cover to advancing troops. It's possible they haven't invented the machine gun yet rather than not needing one, or that they have a different reason for not needing it."

"Regardless," Alexander continued, "population size does influence the nature and frequency of wars. It's puzzling that they engage in warfare at all. Slower development of their weaponry is understandable, considering their circumstances."

"Even so, they've invented missiles," I pointed out.

"Well," Alexander said, "if you think about it, it might be even stranger that we didn't invent them earlier, say before heavier-than-air flight, considering that ancient China was already dabbling in basic rocket technology with gunpowder. In contrast, the idea of the airplane wasn't even conceived until—"

His words were abruptly cut off as we jolted to a halt on a vast steel platform, flanked by four metallic obelisks. We hadn't traveled far, just to the site's perimeter. As it turned out, the platform was another elevator, albeit one with a significantly larger capacity. Hot air hissed from the shaft's edges, accompanying a rhythmic, mechanical pulse as the elevator carried us and the bus underground.

"No, not again," I whispered, anxiety creeping into my voice. "I don't want to go back down."

The elevator plunged us onto a subterranean roadway, wide as a highway, its dim green lighting doing little to dispel the eerie darkness. Massive rusted fans punctuated the tunnel's repetitive stretch every few dozen yards, and several hundred yards farther, we came upon a bridge. Water thundered down its sides in a deafening cascade, the resultant mist engulfing us as we navigated across.

"It's astounding what they've achieved," Alexander said. "Consider the time it took to construct this tunnel alone."

"Slavery can expedite many feats," I retorted.

Crossing the bridge, the bus came to a standstill. At first, I didn't understand why, but then I noticed a small door to our right side. One of the women rose from her seat, baton firmly in hand. She pointed at us and repeated a single word twice. As we stood, she gestured me back into my seat. It seemed Alexander was the one she had indicated. He shot me a puzzled glance as he made his way down the aisle. A soldier exited the bus and unlatched the small door outside.

"Where are you taking him?" I cried out, fully aware my words held no meaning to them, as they led him off the bus. "Alex? Alex!"

"They likely just want to isolate us," Alexander said. "They won't harm us. We're too valuable." Halfway out the door, he turned back toward me. "Don't worry, we'll find each other again."

I pressed my hands against the window, watching them lead him through the door.

"Alex!" I cried out, my voice dwindling to a whisper. "Alex..."

For the first time since our arrival, rage joined my fear. I strained to memorize every landmark, every turn we took, in the hope of finding my way back to that elusive door, should I ever have a chance to escape. Further down the tunnel, Denisovan slaves, their faces a harrowing mask of soot and sweat, stepped aside to let the bus pass. The sight of them stoked my fear of being returned to the mine.

But I wasn't. Instead, we veered onto a smaller side road, guarded by a boom barrier that swung open as a nearby sentry pulled a lever. Ahead lay a spiraling downward path leading to a fortified garage reminiscent of the one from earlier, save for the guards posted at its entrance. *Why was I being transported to such a secured location when Alexander had been whisked away through an inconspicuous door?* I couldn't make sense of it, but my gut churned with ominous foreboding.

Upon disembarking the bus, the air felt acutely colder—or perhaps it was merely the frosty grip of my escalating fear. Engulfed by the looming presence of my captors, I found myself caught in a whirlwind of strange emotions, feeling at once insignificant yet singularly important. I was led inside a facility that radiated a sterile, scientific aura. Its imposing, clinical white walls stood in stark contrast to the personnel's menacing black rubber suits, gloves, and protective masks.

I was taken to an antiseptic room that struck an uncomfortable balance between a doctor's office and an interrogation chamber. Two women stripped me bare and bathed my undernourished frame with a large hose under the watchful eyes of the higher-ups. The frigid water sent a numbing shock through my body. Once they finished, I was left standing in the room's center, arms wrapped tightly around myself, shoulders hunched to ward off the shivers, while they conversed with the women in red.

With teeth chattering uncontrollably, I was finally seated on an examination table while my body was briskly dried with a coarse towel. This, I realized with a sinking heart, was to be my final destination—an underground lab, shrouded from daylight. I found myself consumed by thoughts of my sisters whom I would likely never see again. As the cruel reality of never witnessing them grow up set in, I struggled to hold back my tears.

A few of them eventually escaped, rolling down my cheeks. My examiners leaned in and inspected my face, not with empathy but with indifferent curiosity. One of them reached for a cotton swab and gave it to her colleague, who collected some of my tears with an almost clinical detachment.

I watched them, a question sparking in my mind. *Had weeping evolved as an emotional expression only after* Homo sapiens *diverged from Neanderthals?* I barely had time to entertain the thought, but its allure persisted.

With mechanical precision, they examined my reflexes, heart, ears, eyes, and much to my discomfort, my genitals. The embarrassment aside, it was much like any medical checkup I had experienced before.

While the examiner's superiors conferred with one of them, the other one positioned a camera on a wooden tripod—a model that would be considered old-fashioned back home. She directed me to stand before it, capturing multiple angles of my naked, freezing form. When I attempted to shield my modesty, she approached me, seemingly puzzled by my instinct to cover my private parts. She tapped my arm with her baton, indicating that I was to fully expose myself to the camera. I complied, each flash from the camera ripping away my remaining shreds of dignity.

Following the examination, I was led into a room distinctly circular in shape. Though void of conventional prison bars, it sported a large observation window that chillingly affirmed its nature as a cell. Minimalistic to a fault, it housed nothing but a foldable bed and a cylindrical steel stool, which I soon discerned to be a flush toilet. A soft, white glow bathed the room, emanating from a pair of spherical lamps suspended from the high ceiling.

As I entered, the door locked behind me with a resounding

finality. I approached the window. My captors stood on the other side, their eyes boring into me. One of the women from the airship nonchalantly lit a cigar as she pointed something out about me to the woman next to her. A loudspeaker mounted above the door came to life, its crackling preamble abruptly giving way to a disembodied voice.

"I can't understand you!" I shouted.

Naturally, they knew that. Most likely, they were merely calibrating the system.

I had studied the remains of their species for years, always envisioning them as spear-wielding troglodytes from the Paleolithic era. Now, as they gazed down at my exposed body, dressed in their fancy uniforms, the tables had turned. Here, I was the prehistoric caveman from a long-forgotten past.

The food here was predominantly vegetarian, supplemented occasionally with a sliver of meat. While it certainly beat the worm-infested slop we had been fed in the mine, it still left much to be desired; the vegetables were over-salted and steamed into submission and the meat rubbery and half-cooked. Each morsel led to a disconcerting query: *Was I consuming mammoth or another colossal creature that* Homo sapiens *had wiped out millennia ago in my world?*

My days fell into a predictable rhythm. Each began with a trek to the examination room shortly after I awoke. There, they had me run on an unwieldy treadmill, my skin festooned with electrodes, before sitting me down at a small aluminum table. Armed with a pencil, I was directed to solve a series of puzzles, reminiscent of standard IQ tests that didn't necessitate reading. Their aim, I deduced, was to gauge my physical and cognitive capabilities. Given how typical, or arguably mediocre, I was in all facets of life, I wager they obtained a more representative portrait of my species than they could've ever envisioned.

Post-testing, I was allowed a brief respite on the examination bed before the arrival of two women who, like clockwork, appeared at the same time each day. They employed various means of interrogation, with drawing emerging as the most effective tool. Despite my lack of artistic prowess, I managed to illustrate basic concepts. Their interrogation largely centered around our place of origin and the technology we had carried with us. They continually presented me with the phones—both mine and Alexander's—and pressed me to explain their workings. When I revealed that the batteries had died—something they grasped from my drawings—they found it hard to believe that I lacked the ability to recharge them. Despite their incessant questioning and evident desperation to unearth our secrets, they refrained from resorting to torture. Oddly enough, they seemed concerned about my health, although my weight continued to plummet alarmingly.

Since I didn't know how to charge the phones, all I could do was delve into a broader explanation of the technology to address their inquiries. In one attempt to do so, I drew communication satellites orbiting a globe. Although that was beyond their current level of technology, the idea didn't seem alien to them. If anything, they seemed rather impressed by it, as if they had just begun to think about such things themselves.

During these interrogations, I tried to learn as much as I could about them as well. They didn't mind, as far as I could tell, but rather encouraged my inquiries about their culture and language. They even gave me a pictorial dictionary to study in my cell. Of course, their patience and lack of hostility weren't purely an act of kindness; it was also in their interest for me to learn their language. Regardless, it still fostered in me a sense of respect for them. At this point, I was too weak to see that I, probably according to their plans, had begun developing a mild case of Stockholm syndrome which made me more compliant than I would otherwise have been. I repeatedly reassured myself that my compliance wasn't mere cowardice but a calculated strategy to coax more information from them. Yet, when night fell, it was still I who was imprisoned while they had the freedom to exploit the knowledge I had so readily provided.

Their language was tough to learn, even with the help of the lexicon. I memorized how to spell different words in their alphabet and how to pronounce some of them—such as yes and no. But the only phrases I managed to produce in the end were embarrassingly simple, such as how to say thank you and how to ask for someone's name.

As for where I came from, which intrigued them just as much as our technology, I deliberately lied to keep them from blocking my potential escape later on. However, I did attempt to illustrate the theory of parallel worlds. Using a simplistic diagram of two Earths, I delineated each with outlines of continents. On the first Earth, I depicted two sets of arrows extending toward Europe and Asia from Africa, symbolizing the migratory paths of both Neanderthals and *Homo sapiens*. On the second one, I marked a singular path, representing only their ancestral migration. I then made clear who each Earth represented by pointing.

I couldn't tell how much of this they could grasp, but within days it was clear my explanations had provided them some understanding. They presented me with black-and-white photos of fossils. The images were initially unrecognizable, but the final photo illuminated my understanding: it was an intact skull of an anatomically modern *Homo sapiens*. The sight, under the weight of its profound implications in this world, stirred within me an intermingling of sorrow and gut-wrenching despondency.

The skull appeared to be approximately two hundred thousand years old, hailing from the era when the first *Homo sapiens* arose on Earth. I surmised that our extinction must have occurred sometime after that. *But what catastrophe could have been selective enough to extinguish us yet spare the other hominid species?* My mind circled around the Toba super-eruption* in Sumatra, but that theory crumbled under scrutiny: if a more disastrous eruption occurred in this world, it would have indiscriminately affected all hominid species, possibly driving all to extinction. I speculated on other potential causes as I gazed at the relic of my extinct brethren—a deadly pathogen, an extreme drought...

My musings were cut short as the interrogators unfurled a map of Africa. One of them gestured toward East Africa, likely pinpointing the fossil's origin. Involuntarily, I nodded—a response whose significance to them I couldn't fathom—and focused on the region, scrutinizing it more thoroughly than during our exposure to their world map. To my surprise, a pair of large lakes, though small on the map, were positioned near what would have been Tanzania—my parents' home country—in my world.

Initially, I dismissed them, but as I returned to my confinement later, my thoughts continually strayed back to those misplaced bodies of water. They seemed out of sync with my memory. While geography wasn't my strong suit, my familiarity with this country was substantial. As I pondered more on those lakes, my conviction only deepened; they didn't exist in my world.

I entertained the idea that they were the point of divergence. Perhaps they were craters, signifying an impact event that decimated us before we could migrate from Africa, but after the Neanderthals' ancestors had done so.

* Professor Delsarte notes: About seventy-five thousand years ago, the Toba super-eruption spewed approximately seven hundred cubic miles of magma and rock into the atmosphere, smearing ash all around the globe.

Throughout all this, I yearned to share these revelations with Alexander, but despite my repeated requests for him in their language, they remained obstinately silent, only once assuring me of his wellbeing. I held onto the hope that if I could demonstrate enough of the deference they demanded, they might eventually let me see my friend. *But how much was enough?*

After about two months, I unexpectedly awoke from the lights switching on. Constrained underground, devoid of a clock, the concept of time was elusive. I wasn't entirely sure if the light came on out of schedule, but an inherent instinct told me something was off. Confused, I rose, wrapping my blanket around my waist as I peered into the dimmed, orange-tinged glow beyond the observation window. There, I could discern the lurking silhouettes of Neanderthal researchers and officials. *What could possibly have brought them here at this unusual hour?* A bulky film camera stood on a tripod amidst them, its lens aimed unwaveringly at my cell. They watched in silent anticipation, their cigars glowing like embers in the darkness. My heart leaped into my throat as anxiety took hold of it. *What were they waiting for?* Just as I was about to gesture a question at them, the grating sound of a key in a lock tore my attention away. I swiftly pivoted on my heel and held my breath as I observed the handle rotate slowly and steadily.

A small figure hesitantly stepped into the room—a girl, no more than sixteen. She was clad in a thin, white fabric that did little to conceal her fragile form, and a transparent veil that barely masked the fear etched onto her face. As the door closed behind her, a booming voice echoed from the speakers. The command wasn't for me, but for her. She edged toward me with hesitant, small steps. The gravity of the situation hit me immediately. I bolted toward the window.

"Stop this! You can't do this!" I hammered on the glass, yelling both in my language and theirs. "Get her out of here, please!"

Surprise flashed across their faces. *What had they expected of me? That I would greet this with gratitude, as though it were some kind of gift?* They clearly couldn't comprehend my aversion to the prospect of coerced mating. Casting a glance back at the girl, who now stood frozen in the middle of the room, I rushed to the door, yanking at the locked handle to no avail.

The speakers continued to relay instructions to the girl. She perched on my bed, eyes cast downward at her clasped hands. *Had she been pressured into this situation, perhaps with her family held as leverage, or had she volunteered out of some misguided sense of honor?* Ultimately, it didn't matter whether it was just me or both of us being coerced; the presence of force alone rendered the situation wholly indefensible. Yet, beneath this horrific scenario, a cold logic prevailed. They had evaluated my capabilities, compared my genetic potential with theirs, and clearly decided that a hybrid between our species could potentially outdo the Denisovans.

"You don't understand!" I yelled. "This is a mistake! You'll ruin the very balance of nature!"

I didn't know how to make them understand, or if they would have even cared if I could. Keeping my distance from the girl, I spent the long, harrowing night seated by the door. As the morning approached, the girl moved toward me. She swept some of her unruly, wheat-colored hair away from her face. Her eyes, large and filled with a sadness devoid of tears, spoke volumes. The shallow, hurried rhythm of her breath betrayed her fear, matching if not exceeding mine.

I retreated to the opposite corner of the room as she drew near, a dance that continued for agonizing hours until she finally gave up. She sank to the floor, her back against the opposite wall. That day, neither of us received food or water. They knew what they were doing—no food or water until… Overwhelmed by the futility of it all, I succumbed to tears, pounding on the window in helpless despair.

"She's a child, for God's sake!"

My protest echoed hollowly in the room. It seemed that to these people, her youth was inconsequential, her fertility being their primary concern.

My every move was scrutinized, the researchers diligently noting each reaction. Military officials drifted in and out throughout the day, engaging in casual conversation while observing my frantic attempts to gain their attention. The Neanderthal behind the camera casually lit a cigar, passing the flame to a woman in red who used it for her pipe. Their disinterest in my pleas screamed louder than words. This situation was not up for discussion. Resigned, I slumped down and buried my face in my hands.

For three days, I held out. Both the girl and I were parched with thirst. I clung to the belief they wouldn't allow me to perish, yet my certainty wavered when it came to the girl. Mortal fear flickered in her eyes as she crawled over, pleading. The strap of her dress slipped off her shoulder, unveiling a tattoo of a circle surrounded by three outward-facing triangles. The first piece of art I had seen in this somber world. It might have symbolized the sun or a star, but its true meaning eluded me. I tried to communicate with her, to express my unwillingness for any of this, but only managed to learn her name. Dura.

The act was a torture, tears streaming down my face as I tried to distance myself by focusing on the growing rage toward my captors, silently observing our performance. On the fourth day, they entered and escorted Dura away. I tried to apologize, and although she didn't understand my words, I believe she grasped their intent.

They rewarded my compliance with a generous meal, this time including some fruits. They were unfamiliar, which was unsurprising. The fruits of my world had undergone millennia of domestication and cultivation, so it made sense that another hominid species would foster different ones, even if by mere random circumstances. While they left a bitter aftertaste, their fruits were still a welcome change from my previous meals. But gratitude was a distant emotion; all I could feel was resentment.

I waged a daily war with my memories of Dura, attempting to convince myself that I had been left with no other option. Still, I remained mired in self-blame for what I had inflicted upon her. Rationally, I knew that my actions had saved her from a likely death, but emotionally, I grappled with the weight of my perceived crime. No matter how strenuously I tried to shake them, the haunting images of my actions relentlessly wormed their way back into my dazed mind.

The relentless questioning and examinations proceeded as before, with fresh faces occasionally appearing to probe my mind. I always complied, not to appease them, but out of sheer resignation. I persisted in asking about Alexander, yet each inquiry was met with the same frustrating silence as before. The months trudged on. Thoughts of ending my own life flirted at the edges of my mind as living this way seemed unbearable. However, the sliver of hope that Alexander was alive and needed my help deterred me. Instead, I focused on figuring out how to escape my imprisonment. Thus, each time they took me to the examination room, I tried to find weaknesses in their security. I counted the guards and the doors and tried to devise different plans to escape. But in my debilitated state, and faced with their physical superiority, the odds felt insurmountable. Gradually, a sense of defeat began to creep in, and my suicidal thoughts became increasingly hard to suppress.

In the midst of the monotonous stretch of my captivity, the stillness of what seemed like an ordinary night was ruptured by a gunshot that jerked me awake. A scream followed almost immediately, only to be silenced by a second shot. An eerie quiet settled heavily in the air for a moment. Sitting upright, I strained to listen but could only hear the rasp of my cold breath. Then, the door to my room swung open. A figure swathed in heavy cloaks and veils materialized.

"Who's there?" I asked, reiterating the question in their language.

The figure lunged at me, seizing my arm. Reflexively, I recoiled, fear knotting my muscles tight. But then, beneath the cloak's shadow, I recognized the glint in her eyes. It was Dura. After a moment's confusion, I understood that she wanted me to follow her. In my bafflement, my survival instincts overpowered any doubts, urging me to seize the opportunity.

I quickly draped my bedclothes over my body and followed her into the vacant corridor outside the cell. Dura was armed, her hands gripped tightly around one of the soldiers' firearms. The how and why of her having it was a mystery, but given the circumstances, it was clear she had engineered an escape. A researcher's lifeless body, bathed in a pool of her own blood, lay on the floor. Dura moved with purpose, her determination visible even beneath the shroud of her hood. It was plain her life hinged on the outcome of this breakout. Why she decided to rescue me remained unclear, but I wasn't about to question it. She wielded a stolen set of keys, unlocking doors as we advanced. With each step, the cold bite of the concrete floor seeped through my soles, coursing upward until it clutched at my pounding heart.

Dura stopped short, motioning for me to stand my ground. Voices crackled from a radio somewhere close. She shut her eyes briefly, perhaps contemplating her next move, before hastily cocking the rifle, rounding the corner and pulling the trigger. The echoing shot left my ear ringing, rooting me to the spot in shock until a harsh whisper from Dura stirred me back into action.

I followed her lead into the adjacent hallway where a guard lay, shot precisely between the eyes. Dura scooped up the guard's rifle, checked its load, and handed it to me without a second thought. Its weight caught me off guard, reflecting my own dwindling strength more than its actual heaviness. The moment she pulled the elevator lever, an alarm blared out a repetitive, brassy note and a harsh red light flooded the corridor. Our escape had been discovered. As the elevator began its descent, a flurry of guards appeared. Dura took aim up the shaft, firing at the guards peering down at us from above. To my surprise, they didn't return fire. It struck me that they likely wanted me alive. As Alexander had asserted, we were simply too valuable to them. A flicker of hope sparked within me at this realization, only to be swallowed by the terror pumping through my veins as the platform plunged down the shaft.

As we edged closer to the lower level, where the garage awaited us, Dura tactically positioned herself by hunkering down and aiming the barrel of her rifle ahead. Engulfed by fear, my rational thoughts dissolved, leaving me instinctively seeking shelter behind her like a frightened animal instead of aiding her.

The blaring alarm echoed ominously through the garage where four guards stood waiting. Without hesitation, Dura's finger squeezed the trigger, dispatching one of the guards as she rapidly swung around the corner. I bolted after her. Startled cries erupted from the remaining three guards, who scrambled into pursuit. They unleashed a volley of gunfire that fell off target, probably intentionally sparing me rather than failing to aim. Whirling around, I gripped my rifle close to my belly and fired, catching one of the guards in the leg purely by chance. The recoil stole my breath, reminding me of my inexperience with firearms. Taking cover behind one of the compact vehicles, Dura blasted the door handle off and quickly claimed the driver's seat while firing a second shot at the oncoming guards. I clambered into the passenger side, clutching at the bedclothes wrapped around my body, anxious to keep them from slipping off. As additional guards streamed from the elevator, Dura pressed hard on the gas, ramming the road barrier and leaving them behind. Breathless, I clung to the seat as the car sped toward an unthinkable 100 mph. The engine rumbled and roared like an angry beast, and the tires squealed against the road at every turn, filling the air with the acrid smell of burnt rubber.

With deft maneuvers, Dura veered onto the road leading away from the research facility. Above us, the artificial green glow cast eerie, undulating shadows across our faces while the persistent, trombone-like wail of the alarm echoed around us like an unseen specter chasing us through the darkness.

The door to the room where Alexander had been taken whooshed past us. Frantically, I shouted at Dura to halt, jabbing my finger at the roadside. She briefly took her gaze off the road to cast a puzzled, irked glance my way. Struggling to make myself understood, I stumbled over their word for "friend". Her resolve remained steadfast, however, refusing to divert from her escape route. Clearly, stopping wasn't an option. As the door receded further into the distance, I felt a gut-wrenching sense of betrayal.

"Alex," I whispered to myself. "I'm sorry."

My only consolation was that he had most likely already been transported elsewhere—somewhere akin to my confinement per-haps—and that I would have found nothing behind that door.

The underground bridge from earlier loomed ahead of us, the cascading water on its sides muffling the car engine's furious growl. Dura slammed on the brakes, prompting me to clutch at the dashboard as we spiraled out of control on the slick, treacherous road. Abruptly, we came to a halt at the midsection of the bridge. Dura clambered out onto the wet asphalt, leaving me momentarily confused inside the car. Only when I managed to extricate myself and join her outside did our predicament fully dawn on me.

The dense water vapor cast a misty cloak around us, mak-ing every breath a struggle. Beyond it, a barricade's silhouette loomed ominously on the far side of the bridge, determined to thwart our progress. Dura positioned herself ahead of me, her rifle slung over her shoulder, as she sized up the obscured figures behind the watery curtain.

There was no turning back now. A suffocating dread gripped me, paralyzing my thoughts, as I was unable to conceive a plau-sible path to escape. Yet Dura stood unfazed. With a determined gait, she beelined toward me. I was on the cusp of surrender, ter-ror overtaking me, but her steadfast resolve inspired me to hold on. She grabbed my arm, uttered an indecipherable phrase, and steered me toward the bridge's ledge. Without a second of hesita-tion, she hoisted herself onto it. The cars barricading our path roared to life, their drivers undoubtedly aware of our impending move. By now, it was clear to me too even though I didn't want to believe it. Shakily, I scrambled up next to Dura. As I clasped her small hand tightly in mine, I held my breath and locked my gaze onto her fearlessly determined eyes. And then… we jumped.

We emerged gasping from a balmy underground pool. I pulled myself out of the water, then turned to assist Dura who, weighed down by her soaked garments, could barely keep herself afloat. She still clung to her rifle, but mine had been lost in the plunge. The subterranean lamps above emitted a deep, ultraviolet light, bathing everything in intense, purple hues. I stood frozen, taking in the bizarre spectacle. The room bore an uncanny resemblance to a less opulent Turkish bath, filled with elderly Neanderthal women in various stages of undress. They reclined on carved stones and backstroked lazily through the water, puffing on long pipes. After an initial surge of apprehension, I realized their utter obliviousness to our unexpected intrusion—clearly, their substance of choice had them in its blissful grip.

"An opium den," I blurted out.

Dura limped ahead, her left leg protesting each step. One of the bathers, a burly middle-aged woman, managed to snag her ankle with a feeble grip. Dura instantly swung her rifle into an aiming position but held her fire, seemingly restrained by an internal conflict. The large woman tentatively parted her lips, intending to say something. Sensing this, Dura swiftly rotated her rifle and struck the woman on the head with the butt of the gun, causing her to release her hold. The others started to stir, their befuddled minds slowly piecing together what was happening around them. Dura gestured toward a set of black clothes hanging on the wall, reminiscent of the garb worn by the women in the tower. Hastily, I donned them, including the veil—finally able to discard the tarnished bedclothes. The disguise wouldn't fool anyone for long, but I hoped it would buy me a few extra seconds of anonymity.

A gnarled hand from one of the women landed on Dura's shoulder. With quick action, I detached it and pushed its elderly owner back into the water. We stole away up a narrow stairwell, spilling out into a barren corridor. Our urgency tempered by the need for silence, we navigated the passage as fast as our tiptoes allowed, our soft footfalls echoing off the cold, denim-blue concrete walls. Twisting corridors and stairways gave way to more of the same, a disorienting maze of emptiness. We passed a few off-duty workers who viewed us with mild interest, their gazes lingering more on our state than our identities. Perhaps I had been a well-kept secret, I thought, known to only a select few. Our relative anonymity was short-lived, however.

Stepping into a wide, elongated hallway, we noticed armed guards stationed at the end. Along the walls, rows of barred alcoves housed wailing and protesting Denisovan prisoners, their spirits seemingly still intact after a recent capture. The guards' shouts echoed through the corridor as they spotted us. One hastily grabbed his radio, barking commands into it. Our reflex was to retreat, but the clamor of additional guards approaching from behind halted us. It was a chilling déjà vu—trapped again in a seemingly insurmountable predicament.

Reinforcements joined the guards at the far end of the corridor, advancing toward us. Dura brandished her rifle, her fingers wavering on the trigger. Yet she hesitated, understanding the sheer pandemonium that would erupt if she pulled it—chaos that wouldn't see us making it out alive. The end of our desperate escape seemed inevitable. In the midst of this turmoil, Dura pointed at what looked like a control panel mounted on the wall, just out of her reach. At first, I failed to grasp her intent, not because her gesture was ambiguous, but because my thoughts were a tempest of panic and desperation.

Dura shouted at me, jerking me into motion. I reached for the largest lever on the panel, but her frantic gestures suggested something was amiss. Realization dawned that my choice was incorrect. Taking a moment to study the panel and think was crucial—a challenge that felt Herculean given the pressure. My eyes darted to an array of metal switches adjacent to the lever.

Not pausing to consider their function, I flipped them all in a frenzy. Dura pointed back to the lever once each switch was engaged. It was time to pull it. Despite the brevity of this sequence, time appeared to stretch into eternity. The lever seemed jammed, but it was only my feeble strength opposing me. The soldiers sprinted toward us, bayonets forward, a pair even firing at me. Fear of my impending action had likely overruled their initial orders not to harm me. Bullets whizzed by, ricocheting off the wall next to my head. In a mix of terror and a need to muster strength, I screamed, seized the lever with both hands, and yanked it down with all my weight. It moved with a gratifying thud. I hadn't the faintest clue what the outcome would be, but I didn't have to wait long to find out.

The cell doors, represented by the switches I had frantically toggled, swung open. The imprisoned Denisovans burst forth, their pent-up rage turned against their captors. In the ensuing havoc, Dura snatched my hand as we scuttled close to the wall. A soldier who had escaped the onslaught lunged at me, bayonet aimed at my chest, only to be thwarted by two Denisovans slamming his head against the cold concrete. An alarm wailed overhead, its blatting cry joining the sporadic gunfire echoing in the hallway. Each stray bullet bouncing off the walls sent me into a reflexive flinch. Halfway down the seemingly interminable corridor, we spotted a ventilation shaft near the floor. Dura kicked the duct open and dove in, with me following closely behind. The cacophony of the alarm, the sound of gunfire, and distant screams slowly faded as we forged ahead without a backward glance.

The duct funneled icy air around us, its pitch-black darkness interrupted only by the faint glow seeping through the ventilation grills adjoining the corridors. We came to a vertical shaft, not overly deep but arduous to scale nonetheless. After managing to haul myself onto the ledge, I extended a trembling hand to help Dura, desperately clinging onto what little strength remained. There was a heart-stopping moment as her grip began to falter; panic surged through my veins, prompting me to tighten my hold. With renewed determination, I succeeded in hoisting her up beside me. Now elevated above the ceiling, we discovered that the air vents were embedded in the duct floor, rather than the sides, offering us a glimpse into the patrolled corridors beneath us.

Desperate for silence, I tried to stifle my breath, but the frosty puffs escaping my nose revealed my inability. Every sound we made—the denting of the thin metal under our knees, the occasional scrape of Dura's bayonet against the wall, even our pounding hearts—risked exposing our location. We veered right, distancing ourselves from the hallway beneath, until we found ourselves hovering over a room housing two researchers. Their hunched forms were bent over a large round table, engrossed in something laid out before them. Pausing to get a better look, I was met with a sight that tore through me, wrenching an anguished cry from my lips:

"Alex!"

The researchers raised their heads, surgical masks hiding their expressions. An intense grief squeezed my heart, rooting me to the spot. Strapped to the table like a grotesque version of the Vitruvian Man, Alexander lay exposed, dissected for cold, clinical study. Dura, leading the way, motioned urgently for me to continue. I had no other option but to obey; the researchers were already dashing out of the room, no doubt to summon the guards.

"My God," I whispered, tears coursing down my face despite my efforts to suppress them, "he's dead, he's dead, he's dead."

Was his death an accident, or had they chosen his body for dissection while they focused on probing my mind? Whatever the cause, they were his executioners. Grief gave way to a deep-seated fury, not only toward them but toward myself as well. I was meant to find him. If only I had stepped out of the vehicle when we passed that door in the tunnel, maybe I could've altered the course of events. Instead, I merely watched the door recede into the distance, swallowed by the darkness... and now he was gone.

The horrific image of my friend's desecrated body is forever seared into my memory, yet I can't believe he's gone. I can still hear his voice, an echoing whisper within my skull, speaking of the world that ultimately took him: *There's a certain balance here, you know?*

Despite the unbearable heaviness weighing me down, I trudged on after Dura. We navigated through the ducts, climbing and descending shafts, relentlessly pursuing an elusive safe exit. My hands grew progressively colder with each contact on the icy metal surface, their color fading from a healthy red to a lifeless pale. If I didn't get out of here soon, I realized, frostbite would claim my fingers.

Eventually, we found ourselves in a large ventilation chamber housing a pair of immense, rattling fans. Through the wide gaps between the blades, the mine stretched out menacingly before us. The fans' grating hum drowned out the distant wails of the slaves, but their relentless rotations amplified the musty stench of their plight. They completed one rotation every second—slow enough for a careful escape between the rusted prongs but rapid enough to inflict serious harm if we mistimed our leap.

Dura advanced toward one of the fans, timing her jump with the rhythm of its rotations. The fleeting shadows from the rotating blades danced across her veiled face, casting an intermittent, flickering orange glow. I joined her, my heart pounding in my chest. As Dura prepared to jump, a contingent of soldiers sprinted past us, rifles at the ready. We were forced to wait. Dura's gaze followed the fan's relentless cycles, whispering a countdown under her breath. Then, with no further warning, she sprang forward, emerging unscathed on the other side.

Now it was my turn. Cold sweat trickled down my back. Waiting until readiness struck was a luxury I didn't have; it was a now-or-never moment. I trained my eyes on Dura, timing my jump to coincide with her reappearance amidst the blades. As she emerged before me for the fifth time, I lunged forward. My clothing snagged on something mid-leap, tripping me up, and I landed face-first on the hard, rock-strewn ground, grazing my chin.

Dura extended a hand, pulling me to my feet. The faint clamor of alarms echoed from the direction the soldiers had taken. The enslaved workers, their yellow overalls standing out against the dark rocks, were oblivious to our presence. Their attention was drawn to the distant plateau from which the alarms blared. A commotion was unfolding there—the Denisovans we had liberated were putting up a resistance, buying us precious time for our escape.

A surge of sympathy welled up within me, not only for those embroiled in the distant battle, but for the entirety of their oppressed kind. Their misery knew no bounds. Their sole crime was being of a different species, existing beyond the Neanderthals' sphere of empathy. I couldn't help but wonder about the heart of Denisovan civilization. Here, they were reduced to slave labor, their worth measured by the swings of their pickaxes against the stone. I thought of the mesmerizing Denisovan bracelet[**] discovered in 2008. *If their civilization could create such*

[**] Professor Delsarte notes: The Denisovan bracelet was found in the Denisova Cave nestled within Siberia's Altai Mountains. Oxygen isotopic analysis dated it back to forty thousand years ago, making it the oldest known jewelry of its kind. It was crafted with techniques thought to be too advanced for the Paleolithic era, such as easel speed drilling. The marble bracelet's deep green shade was a testament to the Denisovans' craftsmanship.

beauty and complexity forty-thousand years ago, what marvels could they produce today? My thoughts trailed off, a flicker of hope for this world amidst the despair.

Dura hid the rifle within her cloak and limped forward. The Neanderthal overseers, flicking their lengthy whips to chivvy the enslaved workers back to their toil, were fortunately oblivious to our presence or failed to see through our veils.

We reached a slender path skirting a precipitous cliff. On our right, Denisovans chipped away at the bedrock with burdensome pickaxes, while to our left yawned a canyon of profound depth, the result of a century or more of relentless excavation. The pervasive grime gradually clung to my hands, its gritty particles stinging my throat and infiltrating my lungs. Across the chasm, armed guards methodically examined each face with the beam of their flashlights, undoubtedly seeking us, while their radios murmured a steady stream of chatter. Despite her limp, Dura pressed on without any indication of surrender, though I couldn't discern if she had a destination in mind. However, our consistent upward trajectory did offer me a sliver of hope.

Dura halted. A deep, resonant rumble echoed from above, swiftly followed by the showering of stalactites into the abyss below. I surmised it was the reverberation of a rocket launch—a clear indication of our nearness to the surface. Dura appeared momentarily paralyzed, her eyes darting as her mind seemingly assessed options. A hushed string of words escaped her lips, their meaning lost to me. Then, without missing a beat, she resumed her determined pace. Our only way to the surface seemed to lie with the gargantuan industrial elevators stationed against the cavern walls, yet each was meticulously guarded. Dura's frustration escalated as we weaved our way through the mine, desperation driving us to find an alternative escape route while avoiding detection.

Two guards materialized from the shadows, tailing us at a stealthy pace. However, upon realizing our attempts to evade them, they quickened their steps, forcing us into a frantic run. Gunfire echoed behind us, but Dura kept her rifle hidden, likely deeming it too dangerous to use in such a crowded area. We dashed into a dimly lit portion of the mine, where workers toiled against the stubborn rock face. Our pursuers, their flashlights cutting through the oppressive darkness, remained hot on our heels. We squeezed through a large fissure in the wall, stumbling into a living area—a euphemism for the squalid conditions we encountered.

It was a narrow passage, extending maybe three hundred feet, lined with nooks carved into the walls, each one inhabited by Neanderthal workers. They weren't prisoners like the Denisovans, but their freedom seemed just as limited. Tarnished drapes hung desolately before each room, their futile attempt at privacy rendered almost redundant by the pervasive gloom. Large ceiling diffusers emitted a relentless, high-pitched hum, resonating like a tuning fork—a sonic backdrop that likely echoed in the residents' minds incessantly, day and night. I pondered whether these living conditions had been intentionally designed or if the workers had chiseled out these meager dwellings for lack of a better place to sleep.

Life pulsed through the central artery of the passage, with children playing, meals being prepared, and hushed conversations echoing off the rock walls. Our passage was a careful dance, weaving between bodies and avoiding various obstacles underfoot. I almost tripped over a saucepan of boiling water, my dodge sending a wooden bowl skittering across the floor, eliciting an irked grunt from a shadowed figure crouching next to me. The guards shouted for the throng to clear the path, closing in on us with each passing moment. But to our relief, the miners showed little inclination to comply.

Just ahead of us, the drapery of a nook fluttered open. The dwarf, to whom I had previously offered my bread, stuck his head out, waving fervently. Recognition sparked in Dura's eyes as she returned the wave—an unexpected revelation of a past bond between them. Hidden within the crowded passage, we were a mere breath away from the guards. Dura gave a sharp tug on my cape, a clear signal for me to duck down. Without hesitation, we slipped into the dwarf's compact dwelling. He promptly pulled the drapery back into place. In that cocoon of fabric and stone, we became statues—breath stilled, bodies rigid—as we braced for the worst. It wasn't until the echo of the guards' footsteps grew fainter that we dared to exhale. Dura knelt, gently cupping her friends' cheeks in a tender embrace. At first, I remained silent and watchful, taking in the poignant moment of their reunion that seemed to follow a long separation. Eventually, I slid off my hood and joined them. Dura pointed at me, speaking words beyond my comprehension, although the context suggested an introduction. I spoke my name, and in return learned the name of our host in this squalid home—Sebast.

He sat on his makeshift bed, rolled up his right sleeve and revealed a tattoo identical to the one I had seen on Dura during the night I wished desperately to forget. He then pointed at Dura. Although unsure, I inferred that they were from the same tribe, the tattoo their common emblem. There was a part of me wanting to unravel the story of how I knew his friend, but I lacked the words, and even if I possessed them, the prospect of revealing such a painful memory filled me with dread. What I had done to Dura still steeped me in a sea of shame.

Instead, I opted to share what I could about my origins. To do that, I needed something to draw on. Attempting to articulate my need for paper, I gestured to Sebast. However, my request seemed futile—he was either unable to comprehend my gesture, or simply had no paper to offer. Undeterred, I scanned our surroundings for a solution, my eyes landing on the soot-strewn ground. I smeared my hand in it, using the grime to sketch two circles on the wall behind Sebast's bed, the same illustration I had drawn during my time in captivity. Accompanying the crude depiction with a series of gestures, I hoped to answer some of their unvoiced questions. Their faces, a mix of fascination and confusion, mirrored my own frustration at the language barrier. By the end, it remained a mystery how much of my disjointed explanation they truly grasped.

We remained concealed behind Sebast's draperies for an extended period, the outside noise echoing a melancholy difficult to ignore. I found myself wondering about the lives of these people—if the sun had become a distant memory for them, and whether their children would ever bask in its warmth. The injustice of their predicament struck me hard; they seemed no different from their oppressors, apart from their attire. *Why had these people, innocent men, women, and children, been forced into such a grim existence?* I theorized it must be due to some insignificant, invisible difference—a distinction that my alien perspective failed to comprehend. It was frustrating to stand amongst them, yet remain so ignorant of their histories, their cultures, and their beliefs, so visible to them but utterly obscure to me.

Dura retrieved the rifle concealed beneath her capes, presenting it to Sebast. Their ensuing conversation was fervent. Sebast expressed hope that he might not have felt in a long time, along with a noticeable concern. His fondness for Dura was clear—they could have been siblings, but the truth eluded me as always. After a tender touch to her nose and quick surveillance outside his nook, Sebast signaled it was time to move. Guiding us through a maze of unguarded passageways, Sebast finally halted at a spiraling staircase, presumably leading to the surface. This was as far as he was willing to go. Despite my pleas, he adamantly refused to ascend, seemingly as terrified of the thought of surfacing as remaining in the perpetual darkness below. He whispered something into Dura's ear, possibly a message for their tribe, before turning his apprehensive gaze to me. Acknowledging his assistance, I expressed my gratitude in his native language, after which he silently retreated back into the depths of the mine.

The staircase before us was narrow and gloomy, extending far upward into shadowy heights. In the hushed silence, Dura and I began our ascent, our bodies hunched to accommodate the cramped space. Somewhere midway, the chatter from a radio drifted down to us from above. Holding my breath, I watched as Dura discreetly unsheathed her rifle, settling into a seated position with the weapon primed for action. Our approach hadn't gone unnoticed; the soldier above was ready for us. Pressed against the wall, his form blending with the shadows, he fired his weapon, beating us by a fraction of a second. The concussive blasts from our firearms reverberated within the tight confines of the staircase. Searing pain erupted from my shoulder, marking the journey of a bullet that had found its mark. The soldier, clutching his chest, tumbled down the stairs. I gingerly probed my wound, noting the clean puncture through my shoulder. Yet, whether it was shock or adrenaline, the pain was oddly subdued.

We emerged into daylight from what appeared to be a seldom-used emergency exit. For the second time since my arrival in this world, my eyes struggled to adjust to the daylight. The white tower loomed about three miles away, placing us in close proximity to the launch pad. This was a fortunate circumstance, given that the surrounding area appeared desolate, likely evacuated in anticipation of the recent launch. Deep, sonorous sirens blared from the tower, the pitch lower than the previous alarms—a clear sign of a state of red alert triggered by our audacious escape and the turmoil left in our wake. Two airships hung suspended in the air, their tops dusted with a fresh layer of snow. Surveying the surroundings, I confirmed what I could already feel against my skin: the chill bite of winter had descended.

An isolated parking lot lay a short distance away, occupied only by a lone truck. Likely the transportation of our stairway assailant, it was reminiscent of the vehicles used by the hunters. Dura wasted no time clambering into the driver's seat, a necessity considering our limited mobility on foot. The trouble was, the road led directly toward the tower, not away from it. Nevertheless, Dura brought the engine to life, tossing me the rifle as soldiers began to converge on our position. They unleashed a hail of bullets, but at full speed, we were merely blurs racing past their line of sight.

As we sped alongside the tower, Dura executed a sharp turn that nearly caused the truck to topple. I positioned the rifle through the window and let loose a spray of bullets toward soldiers scrambling into three sleek vehicles, their streamlined contours hinting at high speeds, while their reinforced frames and sturdy build suggested a purpose far more combat-ready than pure velocity. My shots went wide, yet their scramble for cover afforded us some precious time.

With a deafening crash, we broke through the gates of the compound, the guards diving out of our path. Fortunately, it appeared I was still too valuable to be killed on sight, which somewhat lessened the peril of our daring escape. Hot on our trail, the powerful engines of the three vehicles roared. Despite never having laid eyes on it, I recognized that the road stretching ahead was the same route the hunters had used post our abduction. I racked my brain, trying to estimate how long it would take to reach the dirt track where we had been bundled into their truck. I could only hope that I would be able to find it again and that my reduced weight would allow me to squeeze through the opening that had previously proved too narrow. Dura was certainly small enough due to her age. I pondered the risks of bringing her with me. Blending in might pose a challenge for her, I thought, but not an insurmountable one. In the eclectic milieu of modern humans, even her slightly abnormal appearance could go unnoticed, and given her youth, learning a new language and acclimating to a different culture might not be too demanding. Ultimately, I determined that remaining here would pose a far greater threat to her. Since she helped me escape, I owed it to her to save her from this hostile world and to keep her safe—at least until it was safe enough for her to return.

My reverie was broken by the appearance of a woolly rhino lumbering onto the road. Even through the veil of anxiety that shrouded me, the sight was magnificent. Unfazed, Dura maintained our breakneck speed, her eyes fixed on the imposing creature with unwavering resolve. Each passing second ratcheted my nerves taut.

"Unafanya nini?" I exclaimed reflexively in Swahili, my mother tongue. "Turn left!"

Futilely, I gestured with my hand, hoping she would comprehend. But Dura held course, swatting away my desperate attempts to redirect the steering wheel with a stern growl. Just a heartbeat away from collision, she swerved sharply to the left. The abrupt maneuver threw me askew, and in that disorienting moment, I realized Dura had known what she was doing all along. The resounding crash echoed behind us. Risking a glance, I saw our pursuers had met the rhino head-on, one car somersaulting into the air before landing on its roof while the others rolled sideways. The rhino, sacrificed to gain us precious time, lay lifeless on the road.

"That was close," I said, letting out my first relaxed breath since the escape. Probing my injured shoulder, I winced at the intensifying pain. Dura flicked her gaze toward me, her concern palpable as she noted my discomfort.

A stillness lay across the road, only disturbed by the growling engine of our truck. The moon, untouched by human intrusion, hung faintly against the cerulean canvas of the evening sky. As the sun descended, the distant hills rolled into view. Driving up to them, I spotted the dirt path, almost hidden under a blanket of snow, branching off from the main road. Excitement coursed through my voice as I swung around to face Dura. "Over there!" I cried, pointing energetically. "Turn there!" Mustering up what little I knew of her language, I tried to relay the instructions again, praying my fragmented grasp of her words would convey the urgency. A ripple of hesitation passed over her features, and for a heart-stopping second, I feared she would disregard my plea. But, defying my worries, she directed the vehicle onto the dirt road. There was no room for delay. As we veered off the main road, I shot a glance out the window. Two specks were growing larger in the sky, morphing into ominous airships. They were on our trail. We needed to reach the cave in haste, a daunting task given the freezing weather and impending darkness. We abandoned the truck about half a mile from the hills. I gestured our destination to Dura, and side by side, we began our journey through the snow-clad forest. The woodland was eerily quiet, its sounds smothered beneath the snowy mantle. Dura shadowed me as we trudged uphill, looking up at me as if to ask if I was sure about all of this—if she could trust me.

"It's okay," I reassured her, waving her onward. "Go on."

Exhaustion seeped into my bones. My hands were blistered, fingers throbbing against the icy rocks. I mumbled encouraging words to myself as I tried to keep the rifle from sliding off my shoulder. Every step felt monumental. I reached out for a branch to steady myself, only to feel it snap under my weight. I tumbled backward into a cushion of snow, the impact sending waves of pain through my already injured shoulder.

Dura extended her hand, pulling me back to my feet. Reaching the summit felt like an eternity, but once we finally did, we couldn't help but pause, captivated by the vista before us. The sprawling majesty of the Białowieża Forest stood on the brink of darkness, barely clinging to the setting sun's final fiery embrace. The airships, hanging in the sky like enormous beetles, crept ever closer. Soon they would be in a position to spot us from their aerial vantage point. We hastened toward the valley, skidding on the icy cliffs in our rush. Each misstep felt like a breathless dance with danger, but the urgency of our situation spurred us onward.

Once again, I was stricken by the uncanny atmosphere weighing down upon this unearthly place. The knee-deep snow numbed my lower body as we plunged through it. When we finally reached the cave, a sprinkling of stars had appeared overhead. Curiously, the snow seemed to retreat from the cave entrance, likely melted away by the marginally warmer air escaping from within.

Dura's apprehension was tangible as she beheld the petite cave entrance with discernible skepticism. She quivered, her shudders mirroring my own, possibly even exceeding them. Her breaths came out in hurried, shallow bursts. The thought of freezing to death was becoming all too real. To squeeze through the entrance, and more critically, the tighter passage halfway within, we needed to strip down as many clothing layers as possible. My attempts at conveying this necessity to Dura were muddled at best. I could only muster a few uncertain phrases in her language, pointing at our clothes and the cave entrance nestled at the cliff's base. Immobile, likely paralyzed with fear, her gaze fixed on me. As I started to remove her heavy cloaks and capes, I kept indicating the cave, hoping to get the message across. She offered no resistance, but the sorrowful glint in her eyes prompted a moment's hesitation. Her cheeks were flushed from the cold, her small nose adorned with crystallized droplets.

As I peeled away one of her final layers, her eyes darted to her belly. Following her glance, the reality of our situation unfurled before me—she was pregnant. I recoiled, the realization washing over me like a frigid wave. She was bearing our child. My hands trembled as I draped her clothes back onto her. In her condition, navigating the narrow second entrance would be impossible. Even if, by some unfathomable chance, she managed that, the subsequent crawl and climb through the cave would be beyond her. As this grim reality set in, hot tears welled up in my eyes, their warmth a stark contrast against my frostbitten cheeks.

"No, no, no," I whispered, pointing toward the cave with trembling fingers. "It's too narrow. There's no way. You won't fit." My words stumbled out amidst sobbing breaths.

Understanding dawned on Dura's face, reflected in her trembling lower lip, as she pieced together the meaning of my frantic gestures and foreign phrases. It was then I discovered they too could shed tears. A low, haunting drone crept up from above, blotting out the stars with its imposing silhouette. It was one of the airships. Twin beams of intense light swept across the ground from its underbelly. As we huddled together in a desperate embrace, I prayed they hadn't spotted us, and more crucially, that they wouldn't notice the cave.

As we held our breath, waiting for the airship to pass, a torrent of thoughts cascaded through my mind. There was no escaping for Dura—she would be caught. I stood there, rooted in place by fear, marred by weakness. Of all my actions, these are the ones I'm the most ashamed of. She had braved the unthinkable, endeavored to protect herself and the father of her unborn child, and all the while, burdened with the weight of her pregnancy. Yet, I lacked the courage to stand beside her during this pivotal juncture.

With teardrops cascading down my face, I gestured toward the hill, indicating she should retreat to the truck—offering at least a glimmer of hope if they hadn't discovered it. Then, pointing at myself and the cave, I attempted to warn her not to disclose the cave's location to the soldiers should the worst happen and she gets caught. I made a hush sign with my finger on my lips, hoping my rudimentary gestures and scant vocabulary in her language would be enough. There was no way of telling if she understood my desperate charade.

Her thoughts in that moment remain a mystery—whether she accepted my decision or harbored resentment—but urged by my shouts to hurry, she heeded my advice and walked away. Overwhelmed by guilt, I watched her navigate the snow, retracing our steps until she entered a clearing. She paused, looking skyward. Initially, her actions puzzled me. But then, a blinding beam of light illuminated her from above—it was the second airship. Harsh commands boomed down from it, jolting me. An impulse drove me to step forward, but I hesitated, anchored by sheer cowardice and uncertainty about how to save her without us both getting caught. In a haze of remorse and despair, I turned away from her and made my way into the small cave entrance. The haunting sounds of my own sobs were the only companions on my journey back to my world.

I've settled in Hajnówka, a city bordering the forest, and have been visiting the cave every other month. To safeguard its secret, I've fortified the entrance with a formidable boulder—a substantial obstacle if one were to attempt moving it from inside. Additionally, I've arranged branches in a specific pattern that would betray any disturbance. Thus far, it seems Dura has successfully kept the cave a secret. Dura... If she survived, our child would be a year old by now. My thoughts invariably return to them each day, and the regret of leaving them behind gnaws at me incessantly. However, I've found solace in relentless preparations over the past year. Resting on the table behind me are the fruits of my laborious efforts—a collection of assault rifles and semi-automatic pistols, a generous stockpile of matching ammunition, an assortment of grenades, a lone rocket launcher, and a plethora of other deadly instruments. I'm going back. This time, I'll be ready. I'm going to show them the true nature of *Homo sapiens*. They won't know what hit them. I'll give them hell.

Sincerely,
Abasi Hamisi

MY RESPONSE

Paris, Dec. 25th, 20-

Dear Abasi,

The sorrow I feel learning about Alexander's fate is overwhelming. He was a promising individual who didn't deserve such a tragic end. Words can't fully express my emotions. I deeply wish he had shared your joint endeavors with me, allowing me a proper adieu. My heart is heavy for him and for the immense burdens you must be carrying. I want to stress, none of this disaster was your fault. Please, during your times of reflection, free yourself of any unwarranted guilt. Some situations are simply beyond our control or intervention.

The revelations in your letter left me both shocked and skeptical. Honestly, my first inclination was to see your account as a product of an overactive imagination, and I had real concerns about your mental state. However, after thorough verification of the skull you sent, I was forced to reconsider the credibility of your story.

The concept of a portal to another realm is beyond my understanding, and I would argue, beyond our collective scientific knowledge. This revelation might fit with some of the more daring theories in physics. However, I'm convinced that such a groundbreaking discovery would quickly revolutionize most scientific fields in an instant. I say this with all seriousness; if what you describe is true, it would completely change my long-held beliefs about the universe. The mere existence of a gateway to this parallel Earth is profound enough. As for the wonders and terrors you discovered beyond... If proven true, they have the potential to fundamentally alter the framework of my research.

It brings some comfort to know you came out unharmed, and I am deeply grateful for your willingness to share your experiences with me. That you chose to reveal such profound information to me, among all your acquaintances, is highly meaningful. I've thought extensively about the advice I could give, and I sincerely hope you are still in a position to receive it—still residing in our world, so to speak. My initial thought was to suggest seeking the help of authoritative bodies to assist in recovering your child. However, after more reflection, I realized something you've probably already considered: any government, faced with such a discovery, would inevitably seek to control this newfound realm. Their actions would likely reflect the imperialistic tendencies of our ancestors, exploiting and claiming every piece of land, thus condemning the Neanderthals to extinction—repeating the ancient tragedies our predecessors inflicted on our own Earth.

However, I strongly urge you not to return to that realm alone. Even with advanced weapons at your disposal, you're still just one person against their vast numbers. While your desire for retribution is understandable, I beg you not to act solely on emotion. Find a reliable ally and take all necessary precautions to ensure the safety of both your child and its mother. But please, don't let the desire for revenge consume their entire world for the wrongdoings committed solely by their tyrannical leaders. I await your reply with bated breath, the anticipation growing with each passing moment.

Veuillez agréer, monsieur, l'expression de mes salutations distinguées,

Nathalie Delsarte

THE SECOND LETTER

Dear Prof. Delsarte,

I'm once again back from the dreadful world where humankind never managed to escape its cradle. The gravity of my situation lingers, yet, at present, there is no immediate threat to my life. So, I've decided to seize this transient moment of reprieve, and any other opportunities when I can write, to document my experiences since our last communication.

Roughly a year ago, shortly following your response, I removed the boulder obscuring the cave's entrance and ventured back into its depths. My goal wasn't to immediately cross to the other side, but rather, to lay the groundwork for doing so. The initial step involved a careful expansion of the entrance leading into the midway chamber. Armed with nothing more than a small hammer and a flat chisel, I painstakingly chipped away at the rock to enlarge the opening without attracting undue attention. I had bulked up, my physique fortified with added muscle mass, which necessitated this enlargement. It would also facilitate the transportation of my equipment. Although

I dedicated nearly ten hours daily to the task, often pushing myself until my hands bled, progress was slow, and despite my best efforts, the final result was still a challenging crawl.

I established a provisional base within the midway chamber, stocking it with supplies, medical aids, electronics, and weaponry. Some items, including a pair of hexagonal drones and a heavy machine gun, were too bulky and required disassembly for transportation into the chamber. The task of carrying this equipment through the cave was a slow and tedious process, and I narrowly avoided detection on my nightly excursions to the valley on several occasions.

Navigating this phase alone was a significant burden, and your suggestion to include companions echoed persistently in my thoughts. Despite my superior arsenal, venturing solo would leave my chances of survival woefully inadequate. However, sourcing suitable companions presented its own considerable challenge, as the ideal candidates would need to fulfill at least four criteria—an open-mindedness to my extraordinary tale, loyalty to me, the right set of skills, and the motivation to join me. These attributes were unlikely to coexist in one person, but having finished setting up camp in the midway chamber and after further contemplation, I resolved to seek such individuals.

Relying on strangers, such as mercenaries, was out of the question—I lacked both the means to compensate them and, more crucially, the ability to place my trust in them. Thus, I had to turn to my circle of friends. This decision weighed heavily on me, considering the fate that befell Alexander. The last thing I wanted was to endanger another loved one. I struggled with my conscience over this for a long time and even though I lost that battle, I still reached out the only two individuals from my acquaintances who somewhat fulfilled my criteria.

Even though they regarded me as trustworthy, I was certain

they wouldn't believe my full account without corroborative evidence. Thus, I presented them with a diluted version of my experiences, leaving out the most incredulous parts. I simply told them I had found something worthwhile exploring further and attached some photos of the cave. Just enough to pique their interest and convince them to travel to Hajnówka to see the cave for themselves. I was certain that once they witnessed what Alexander and I had discovered, they wouldn't hesitate to join me. And when they finally laid their eyes on the valley on the other end of the cave and I could fill them in on all the details of my story without fearing being shunned, their reaction was as predicted—one of overwhelming bewilderment and fascination.

"Unbelievable," Larissa breathed, looking up at the alternate March sky and the towering, bud-bursting trees. "I'm at a loss for words, Abasi. This is utterly incredible!"

As a decorated physician for Médecins Sans Frontières, her credentials alone made her a vital addition to our expedition. But it was her insatiable spirit of adventure that truly drew me to her—she thrived on challenges like cave exploration and mountain climbing, a trait that I had observed firsthand when we met a few years earlier.

"Staggering," was all Jacob managed. "So this isn't Earth, but some parallel world, huh? I admit, I thought you'd lost your marbles when you started talking about this mysterious cave. But man, you didn't disappoint. And now you're telling us there are Neanderthals here? And that they killed your friend and forced you to do the deed with one of their girls? That's just… I mean that's just—"

"Insane," I finished for him. "I know."

Jacob was a childhood friend. Our paths had diverged years

ago—he pursued a career in the military while I immersed myself in academia—yet our bond endured. His military training, coupled with an innate fascination for firearms, made him an invaluable asset for this undertaking. However, his most defining attribute was his unwavering loyalty. Although we no longer spent as much time together as we did in our youth, and even though we didn't have that much in common as adults, he still felt like a brother to me.

We returned to the midway chamber following our brief jaunt into the alternate world, a journey undertaken solely to validate its existence for my friends. There, amidst the echoes of our awe and speculation, we spent considerable time crafting a strategy. I had roughly marked the suspected location of the subterranean labor camp on an old map of western Belarus. Reflecting my friends' dauntless dispositions, they were both eager to explore, but neither had anything to gain from risking their lives to save Dura and our involuntary child. I could only hope their sympathy, perhaps coupled with gratitude for being part of this monumental discovery, would sway them to my cause. Instead of asking directly, fearing their reactions would be equally direct, I subtly communicated my desperation through the discussion of what I wanted to do.

"Man, this is heavy," Jacob remarked after I had finished speaking, my sentences stumbling over each other in the process. "Are you sure you don't want to loop in the military? I get not wanting this secret to fall into the wrong hands, but maybe the right organization could help you out responsibly, even help you get payback. Think CIA, or, heck, even the UN? Besides, there's a bigger picture here, right? We always talk about not having a Planet B, but here it is!"

Larissa vehemently shook her head. "That'd be a grave error. This planet, this second Earth, belongs to its inhabitants. The moment any government from our world gets wind of it, they'll bend over backward to exploit it. We'd witness the dawn of a new era of colonialism, fueled by our world's desperate quest for resources we've squandered. They'd shed as much blood, if not more, as in previous conquests. We need to keep this to ourselves."

"But they aren't humans," Jacob said, "and they don't strike me as peaceful themselves. They seem cruel, vicious even. I mean, come on—humanity first. Is that such a controversial statement?"

"Personally," I said, "I count all members of genus Homo as human and—"

"That's irrelevant," Larissa cut in, "They're sentient beings!"

Jacob held up his hands in surrender, "Easy now, just throwing a suggestion on the deck. I'm no fan of history repeating itself either. The last thing I want is to kick off some blood-soaked gold rush. But let's face it, we're a three-man team squaring up against an army of Neanderthals. I thought it would be worth at least discussing how to level the battlefield."

"Trust me," I said, "I've spent a lot of time thinking this over and I have to say, I agree with Larissa. We also have to consider what a government organization might do if they found out about this. They could shut us down, send us home, or even keep us captive. That's why I've only brought this up with the two of you. I trust you both and I know you're capable. I realize I'm asking for a lot and I don't want you to feel pressured."

Jacob squared his shoulders, "No need for the pep talk. I'm with you all the way. You trust me, I trust you. Simple as that." He then shifted his gaze to Larissa, "You in? Just the three of us?"

"If within our means, of course." She turned toward me. "I owe you nothing less, Abasi. But let's be clear, it's not guaranteed to be within our means. I want to help. I know you hoped I would when you invited me, but we have to stay realistic. We need to determine whether there's even a feasible plan to make this work."

Jacob raised an eyebrow, "So, you're in, then? We'll need a damn good strategy, no one is denying that."

Larissa nodded, "Of course, we should help the girl, and others caught in their regime if we can—but only as long as we're not walking blindly into a suicide mission."

Jacob's willingness to help was no surprise. He had always been ready for a chance at heroism. As for Larissa, I didn't know her well enough to predict her reaction with certainty. So, discovering her openness to the idea brought a wave of relief over me. The conversation shifted toward strategizing our plan of action. Jacob was the first to lay out his thoughts:

"We're at higher risk of detection or worse, getting killed, if we overstay our welcome. This is a straightforward rescue mission... Well, straightforward might be stretching it, but you catch my drift. We're not trying to settle here, but to save someone. What you want is a quick in-and-out. At least, that's what I recommend, drawing from my personal experience."

His suggestion hung in the air for a moment as I pondered it. But before I could articulate my thoughts, Larissa chimed in:

"Your plan seems hasty. Neither Abasi nor I are soldiers. Given our limited experience, your approach seems fraught with danger. I propose a diplomatic strategy more in line with our strengths. Let's seek allies, using goods as gifts to build trust or as trade for their support."

Jacob countered, "Alliances? How do we determine who's trustworthy? My recommendation is to survey the area around the site, identify a covert entry point, free some of the slaves, and then leverage the ensuing chaos—maybe gaining some friends along the way. Granted, you two aren't soldiers, but with our superior weaponry, you should be well-equipped to handle them."

"We don't even know where they are keeping Dura," I said. "I concur with the need for quick action once we've located her and that we should heed your advice for that phase. However, beforehand, we need detailed intelligence on what we're up against. To gather that, we may need to liaise with the Neanderthals, like it or not. Not all of them are hostile. It appears that Dura's people were at odds with the ruling faction."

Larissa offered another perspective, "What if we made contact with the Denisovans as well? You managed to help a few of them escape during your last visit. Maybe they'd be open to assisting us if we demonstrate our intentions are aligned with theirs."

"I'm not sure," I responded. "In the depths of that horrendous mine, where they were enslaved, they'd likely grab any opportunity for escape, and I'd be eager to provide it. But we lack knowledge about their society, and reaching them would require us to traverse all the way to the Urals. Our greatest prospect for allies likely lies with Dura's people."

Larissa conceded, "That's reasonable."

"Do you believe the girl's people would gamble their lives to help us free the prison camp?" Jacob queried. "And would you be able to communicate that request?"

"I hope to—" I started, but Larissa interjected.

"Could we possibly leverage diplomacy to avoid conflict entirely?" Jacob was poised to argue, but Larissa held up her hand, her voice firm. "At least consider my proposal. If we could establish a presence here, maybe team up with Dura's tribe as we've discussed, and offer something of value to the Neanderthals in power, they might agree to a trade. Perhaps we could negotiate for the girl and the child."

Jacob leaned back, crossing his arms. "But from Abasi's account, the only thing they might want is something that would give them the upper hand in their war against the Denisovans. Trading weapons with an enemy, in my opinion, is tantamount to shooting ourselves in the foot."

Larissa wasn't deterred, "True, but what if we figure out what they value for themselves? If we understand what holds currency in their society, we might be able to bribe a guard or an officer who has access to Dura. I'm simply suggesting there are alternatives to violence and we should explore them, no matter how implausible they might seem, rather than defaulting to force."

Jacob responded with a sardonic grin, "Your idea isn't just improbable, it's downright impossible. Can you imagine bribing some random soldier in our world, or even a high-ranking officer, to free a prisoner of great value to a nation's war effort? You would have to bribe an entire chain of command! No, large-scale trade of knowledge and technology is the only plausible diplomatic approach, and again: do we really want to put our own advantage in the hands of the enemy?"

Ultimately, we agreed to proceed one step at a time, starting with setting up a concealed campsite in the heart of the valley. We carried only the essentials needed for reconnaissance, leaving the remainder of our supplies hidden within the cave to avoid detection during our absence.

After securing the secondary camp, it was time to survey the surrounding area. We swapped our caving gear for tactical clothing—sturdy boots, heavy-duty jackets—and armed ourselves with holstered Glocks and AK-47s in hand. The reassuring weight of the rifle sent a rush of confidence coursing through me. While our main objective remained rescue, I couldn't ignore the simmering desire for vengeance swelling within me.

"Remember, shoot to kill only," Jacob advised as he attached hand grenades to his belt. "Despite advocating for a forceful approach, I'm not oblivious to the destructive power of firearms. Treat them as lethal every time you use them." His gaze bore into me, as if sensing my turbulent emotions. "In simpler terms, only use them if you're ready to take a life—and that should be a rare circumstance. Understood?" His attention pivoted to Larissa. "Remember, keep your fingers off the trigger unless you're prepared to use it."

"Don't worry about me," Larissa retorted. "I know the basics."

"Never underestimate women," I said, grinning. "Especially not in this place."

"I've had my six covered by countless brave women in combat," Jacob said, annoyed at my remark. "Never had a pacifist in the mix though."

Larissa chuckled. "Who said I was a pacifist? My point is that violence should be the final option when all else fails. You seem to treat it like any other tool."

"I ain't sayin' that," Jacob countered. "But there're times when it's the quickest route to a solution. We can't ignore that, getting bogged down by some hippie ideals. Back in Afghanistan, the Taliban had a whole village under their thumb. The villagers, amicable folks, had lent us a hand previously. Somehow, the Taliban sniffed that out. Every few hours, they'd pick a villager, didn't matter man or woman, and execute them in plain sight. Sure, we could have sought a peaceful resolution. We might have called in a negotiator, hammered out a deal. Violence wasn't the only option. But it turned out to be the most effective. We smoked those bastards out, sent them tail-between-legs back to their holes. We pulled a whole load of folks out of the fire that night, folks who'd have been lost if we'd acted according to your playbook."

"An act of heroism, no doubt," Larissa responded, "but who holds sway over that village now, with the war done and the gallant Americans gone?"

"That's not the point!" Jacob barked. "If you'd been in my boots—"

"Let's press on," I said, striving to defuse the tension. "We've got a lot of terrain to cover before nightfall."

Their argument trailed along as we climbed the hill, but it ceased abruptly when they took in the vista of the vast, unspoiled forest. This was the moment when the gravity of our situation transitioned from a mere abstraction to an undeniable reality in their minds.

"What's that?" Larissa queried, her finger pointing eastward.

My eyes followed her gesture to a massive plume of smoke billowing skyward on the horizon.

"That must be the place they held us captive," I said, my voice reflecting my shock. "It's ablaze!"

"What could've happened?" Larissa asked. "Do you think it was attacked?"

"I'm not sure," I responded. "It's certainly possible."

I stared at the rising smoke. From this remote vantage point, where the only sound was the whisper of trees swaying in the gentle breeze, it all seemed deceptively serene. Yet, the turmoil hidden from view still touched me, implanting a sense of foreboding in my heart.

"Judging by the dense black smoke," Jacob said, "it's a high-intensity fire, feasting on heavy fuels." He lifted a pair of binoculars to his eyes, adding, "Can't confirm from this distance, but I'd wager it's burning human... or should I say, Neanderthal-made materials. Structures, vehicles, that sort. Definitely not a natural incident."

"This changes things," I said.

"Are you suggesting we head that way?" Larissa asked. "Straight into a raging fire?"

"We'd have the element of surprise," Jacob retorted. "Arriving post-dusk, before the fire's extinguished, could give us a closer inspection of the enemy without risking capture."

"I'm inclined to agree," I said. "Let's scout it out. We can maintain a low profile nearby."

"I think we should stick to the plan," Larissa argued. "How do we know that fire hasn't been burning for days already? We shouldn't be hasty. Let's explore—"

"Negative," Jacob said. "We should—"

"God, you don't have to talk like that." Larissa rolled her eyes. "You're not on active duty."

Jacob flashed a grin. "Once a Marine, always a Marine. Look, I'm just saying we should leverage this situation. If they're pre-occupied handling a disaster of some kind, they're less likely to notice a few *Homo sapiens* snooping around."

"Who knows," Larissa said. "They might mistake you for a Neanderthal."

Their banter continued as we made our way back to the campsite to weigh the situation more thoroughly. I settled onto a rock adjacent to our tent, watching as Jacob and Larissa squared off, their stance hinting at a simmering tension.

"Look, it's possible to be excessively cautious, too," Jacob stated. "I'm not saying we should just—"

"Exactly how is it being overly cautious not to charge head-long into a warzone?" Larissa cut him off, turning to me, "Abasi, what's your take?"

"I hate to say it," I said, "but I side with Jacob on this. It's a window of opportunity, and we don't know how long it will be open." Larissa looked away, covering her forehead with her hand and giving a disheartened shake. "Listen," I continued, "you haven't witnessed what I have. That place… it's a pit of misery, despair, and death. It's darker than your worst nightmares. An unending starless night. You don't have to accompany us, I wouldn't fault you in the slightest, but if the slaves have risen, or if they're being freed… In that case, I need to be present. I need to be a part of it. This isn't just about Dura… or even the child. It's about all of them. If I can lend them aid now—possibly during their most critical moment—I believe I should. Going there might also let us forge the alliances we were discussing earlier. All I'm trying to say is…" I paused, grappling for the right words. "If you had seen the depths of suffering these people have endured, I think you too would be willing to shoulder some risks to assist them in their fight for, not just survival, but for freedom as well."

"That's exactly it," Jacob chimed in, a proud smile tugging at his lips as he looked at me. Turning back to Larissa, he added, "You simply can't understand unless you've witnessed the victims' distress as they face or flee their oppressors. It makes your blood boil, and you just know you have to do something. Merely marching through city streets with protest signs doesn't cut it. Sometimes you just—"

"You don't know me." Larissa fixed Jacob with an unflinching gaze. "You don't know what I've seen, what I've experienced. I've encountered horrors you can't imagine, and more often than not, they have been the direct consequence of men's eagerness to charge into battle. Let me paint *you* a picture." She took a brief pause, her gaze momentarily flickering to the moss beneath her feet. Gathering her thoughts, she proceeded in a hushed tone. "I was part of a medical relief team that arrived in the aftermath of a Boko Haram raid. A group of schoolgirls had been liberated, but at a cost. I arrived on the scene right after the battle, and what I saw was a nightmare. The ground was littered with bodies, the air thick with the smell of gunpowder and blood. But that was something I was trained to handle. However, among the survivors, there was one girl… one girl who needed more than just stitches and antibiotics." Larissa's eyes, filled with memories too painful to articulate, glistened as a tear escaped. With a quick swipe, she cleared the moist trail off her cheek and continued her narrative. "In the midst of that grim landscape, there was no time to wait for an operating room or proper medical facilities. The girl had been shot in the head and was heavily pregnant. The baby… the baby needed to come out, right there, right then." She inhaled deeply, steadying her voice, the faintest tremor betraying the impact of her reminiscence. "I performed a C-section, right there in the blood-soaked dirt, using whatever rudimentary tools we had at our disposal. I thought… I believed there was a chance for the unborn child, that it wasn't too late." A solemn silence hung in the air as she finished, her voice barely a whisper, "But the baby didn't make it. And neither did the girl… All that effort, all that hope, and all I was left with was a lifeless child in my arms and a mother who never got to hear her baby cry. That's the reality of war. It doesn't just take away lives; it crushes hope and leaves scars that never heal. So, yeah, I think I'm qualified to say violence should be avoided when possible."

Jacob's mouth opened slightly as if to respond, but no words came. His hardened expression softened momentarily, revealing a glimmer of understanding.

"Be that as it may," Larissa continued, redirecting her attention toward me. "I think we should go. You made a good point about helping them now when they may need it the most. But first, let's eat something, shall we? We can't tackle the challenges ahead on an empty stomach."

We set about preparing a meal over our camping stove. My

hand quivered as I lifted my fork, the realization that I was returning to the scene of my own torment dawning on me. Each time I blinked, harrowing visions of Alexander's lifeless form on the autopsy table, or Dura's stark expression as I left her behind in the cold for my own survival, flashed in my mind.

"You holding up okay?" Larissa asked, her hand gently steadying my wrist to halt the trembling. "You sure you can handle this?"

"I'm okay," I said, "I mean, I will be okay. It's just… Since I came back to our world my experiences have felt a bit like a nightmare—something that didn't really happen. And now I suddenly have to come to terms with the reality of it all."

Jacob studied me, his gaze thoughtful. "I can spot PTSD when I see it. It's a brutal, crippling condition. Normally, it'd be a no-go to take someone suffering from it into a combat scenario—they can be unpredictable—but our situation, it's different. Still, you need to ensure you can hold it together. And remember, you've got us watching your six. You aren't alone this time."

Finding the dirt road wasn't much of a challenge, even though nature had begun to reclaim its edges. The journey ahead was a day's hike, and to remain undetected, we were forced to weave our path through bush and thicket, off the beaten road—slowing our progress considerably. When we reached the main road, poised to use it as our compass, two imposing trucks thundered by, forcing us to drop low into the undergrowth. Heart pounding, we held our breath and waited several minutes before daring to rise again.

"Seems they're in quite a rush," Larissa noted, her voice carrying a tinge of unease. We remained standing in the middle of the broad road, our eyes tracing the receding forms of the trucks. "I would really want to know what's going on over there," she continued. "Something about this doesn't sit right with me."

The spring sun struggled to pierce the plume of smoke billowing on the horizon, rendering it a mere pale disc in the sky. Intermittent rays managed to break free, glinting off the retreating trucks. I shared Larissa's unease, but not for the same reasons. Her concern was rooted in the uncertainty of the unknown; mine, in the dread of the known. *What did all this mean for Dura and our child?* Shaking off my thoughts, I looked at my companions, took a deep breath, and said with determination:

"We need to get off this road and keep pressing forward."

The raw, untamed wilderness around us felt as menacing as the open road, tightening its grip on our nerves with each step we took. Yet, it was the awareness of our precarious situation more than the landscape that made our palms sweat and our hearts hammer against our chests. To the naked eye, the scene was deceptively serene—just another mild spring day, not unlike what we'd have experienced back home, albeit early in the year. Larissa voiced this sentiment while examining a pinecone:

"It's the similarities, more than the differences, that make this place so unsettling. I could snap a picture right here, even of that road constructed by hands not of our kind, and show it to folks back home, and they wouldn't spot anything amiss. And yet, this is the most foreign place anyone from our world has ever set foot in. The scale of cognitive dissonance I'm experiencing... it's off the charts. It's just... well, unnerving, to put it mildly."

After some time, with the sun barely hanging onto the edge of the sky, we were hit with the sharp, sour smell of burnt rubber. Given our proximity to its source, we resolved that lingering near the road was too dangerous, and hence, we pressed further into the dense forest. The plume of smoke stretched out directly above us, its serpentine trail marking the path we needed to follow. As we approached its origin, we slinked stealthily to the forest's edge, easing through the grass before pulling out our binoculars for a closer inspection. Flames consumed nearly every building, sparing only the stark white tower. A rocket stood desolate on its launch pad, seemingly forgotten. I saw no signs of activity until Jacob silently gestured to something about half a mile to our right. Squinting through the binoculars, I adjusted the focus. Two figures in rubber suits and gas masks brandished flamethrowers, unleashing a torrent of fire into a hole in the ground. The heat around them caused the air to ripple and warp, obscuring a clear view amidst the smoky twilight.

Jacob broke the silence with a solemn murmur. "That's a mass grave. Look at the bodies piled up next to it."

We followed his gaze, and I noticed the familiar yellow overalls. "Denisovans," I whispered, my voice a mere thread in the wind. "Those bodies—they're Denisovans."

Larissa's response was equally quiet, a murmur of conclusion, "They must have quelled the uprising."

Horror strangled my response, as my eyes took in the chilling sight. One of the figures—probably a Neanderthal soldier—started throwing bodies into another pit. A truck rolled up, possibly one of the vehicles we had noticed earlier on the road, and it disgorged more corpses onto the mound. A patchwork of yellow overalls interspersed with women's clothing. One body even sported a red uniform.

"Women," I uttered. "It doesn't make sense. Burying their own alongside the slaves… their superiors with their enemies?"

"Perhaps they don't possess the same sensibilities as we do," Larissa suggested.

"No… Or, I mean, it's possible," I said, "but during my time here, the Neanderthals appeared deeply concerned about such matters. This seems incredibly out of character."

"They're tossing the bodies like they're trash," Jacob noted. "And that protective gear? Just for the fire, or what?"

"I've never seen them wear anything like it before," I said. "We'd need to get closer to get a clear look of what's going on."

We withdrew into the forest, skirting the site to find a better vantage point. My grip tightened around my weapon as we stealthily moved through the verdant, albeit ashen, foliage. With each step, every rustle of leaves against my legs, and each twig snapping beneath my boots, a jolt of dread surged through me. Being in such close proximity to that hellish place—a monument to my suffering—rattled my resolve, yet the sight of it ablaze, the decorated uniforms amidst the bodies, kindled a grim satisfaction within me, despite our ignorance of the cause behind the conflagration.

Larissa grabbed my arm, freezing me mid-step. From behind, Jacob whispered, "I see it, too. We've been spotted."

"S-see what?" I stammered. "I can't see anything."

"We're being watched," Jacob said. "I reckon there's a temporary camp not far off."

"Wh-what's our next move?" I questioned, scanning the area, though nothing seemed amiss.

"Get low," Jacob directed, nudging me swiftly behind a hefty fern, which sent a flurry of ash spiraling from its leaves. "They've been tailing us. How many did you spot, Larissa?"

"I'm uncertain," Larissa admitted. "Two behind us, at least three ahead."

"Clever devils," Jacob said. "They're trying to encircle us."

We made a break in the only direction we could—toward the raging inferno. Jacob led us with swift, zig-zagging maneuvers, his hand often motioning for us to stay low. Given the Neanderthal's intimate knowledge of the terrain and their keen sight in the dimming evening, it seemed an impossible task to slip away. Our only edge was our arsenal.

"We won't be able to outrun them forever," I said.

Jacob raised an eyebrow. "You suggesting we stand our ground?"

"I'm not sure," I responded, hesitating. "Maybe using one of the grenades would throw them off?"

Larissa chimed in, "It might buy us some time to find a safer spot."

Without waiting for further input, Jacob hurled a grenade. The ensuing explosion sent birds flapping away, their frantic silhouettes cutting through the sky. Seizing the moment, we took several unexpected turns. After some distance, we paused to regroup and felt a momentary relief, believing we'd lost them. But our respite was fleeting. Glancing around, it became clear we'd inadvertently entered the site's perimeter. With the distant growls of their hunting dogs reaching our ears, we felt more trapped than before. Retreating didn't seem viable, so we pressed on, hoping the unfolding chaos would cloak our presence.

The heat from the burning buildings stung our faces as we approached them. We traversed a parking lot strewn with the charred remnants of cars and continued past a signboard that showcased a Neanderthal skull underscored by a thick red line.

"That's a rather foreboding sign," Larissa whispered. "Most certainly a warning of some kind."

"Hold on," Jacob commanded, focusing on a distant activity. "What's happening over there?"

Two soldiers, identical in attire to the ones wielding flamethrowers, corralled a trio against a wall, their hands bound behind them. They aimed their rifles at them. We stood motionless only three or four hundred feet away, covered by the darkness and the rubble around us, and watched. The figures against the wall—two men and one woman—were unmistakably Neanderthals, their unique features catching the glow of the fires.

Only one of them donned a yellow overall; the other two were clad in military garb.

"This isn't an uprising," I said. "This is something else, something—"

Jacob nodded toward the captive Neanderthals. "They don't seem well."

Despite the darkness, their deteriorating condition was evident. Pallor washed over their faces, and one of the Neanderthals in military attire, who appeared to be a former soldier, coughed persistently while pleading for mercy. His imminent executioners seemed conflicted, their movements hesitant, reluctant about the grim task at hand.

"They're sick," Larissa observed. "Could they be—" The chilling click of the rifles being primed interrupted her. "We can't just watch them die," she insisted. "This is our chance. Rescuing them aligns with our mission, and they might aid us in return. I doubt we'll make it out here on our own."

Jacob hesitated, "I'm not sure if—"

"Now or never," I cut in.

Jacob nodded, resolve hardening in his eyes. "Alright. Let's go."

We caught them off guard. Emerging from the shadows, we moved into the glow of the nearby flames. Jacob discharged a warning shot into the air. The soldiers spun around, their expressions betraying confusion, and trained their rifles on us. They looked at each other back and forth, clearly unaware of our species' existence, and decided to surrender their rifles, perhaps more afraid of the red dots of our laser sights than the warning shot. The woman they were about to execute started shouting, gesturing vehemently toward us, seemingly ordering the soldiers not to relent. She must've recognized me. It was astonishing to see her try to direct her own would-be executioners. Yet, in the face of our show of force, they didn't dare comply with her commands. Seething with rage, I advanced toward her, keeping my rifle aimed at her.

"Abasi, what are you doing?" Larissa hissed. "Don't be foolish. Come back!"

"Quiet!" I yelled at the Neanderthal woman. "Where's Dura? Tell me! Dura!"

She met my eyes with a scornful gaze. Dried blood streaked from her ear, marring her pale complexion. I shouted again, now in her tongue, only to be met with silence. It infuriated me, but then I realized she probably couldn't hear me. Beside her, one of the men exhibited similar signs, his ears swathed in bandages, likely afflicted by the same ailment. The distant sound of a volley of gunfire pierced the air, and the muffled, frantic cadence of the soldiers' breathing intensified behind their masks, their radios buzzing with aggressive chatter.

"We need to move, and fast!" Jacob urged, keeping the soldiers in his sights. "Reinforcements will be here soon."

"I want you to see this," I said, pointing out their ear condition to Larissa.

"It looks like a severe otitis," she noted, "an ear infection or inflammation."

"Enough talk!" Jacob snapped. "Do we trust the captives or not?"

"I don't know," I said. "I say we untie the one in yellow first. He's a former slave."

"Do it!" Larissa said. "There aren't any other options. We need them."

The woman writhed in panic upon seeing my intentions. The man struggled to his feet after I had set him free. While not as visibly sick as the others, he clearly wasn't in good shape either. As he found his footing, a violent cough nearly toppled him. Recovering, he promptly picked up one of the weapons discarded by his former masters.

"Whoa!" Jacob shouted, training his rifle on the freed man. "What's he up to?"

"Hold on," I said. "Let's see what he does."

We watched, breaths held, unsure if he would turn hostile. To my shock, in a swift, decisive movement, he drove the bayonet into the woman's throat. I wanted to intervene, to tell him I needed her alive, but everything happened too quickly. Larissa averted her eyes in horror as the woman choked on her own blood. Likewise stunned, Jacob momentarily lost focus. Seizing the moment, the masked soldiers quickly vanished into the shadows. The man we had just freed gave chase, his pursuit marked by gunshots that echoed among the flaming structures.

"Untie the other one!" Larissa instructed.

"Be ready," Jacob warned. "If he tries anything, I won't hesitate."

I approached the remaining captive with caution, fearing he wouldn't be as grateful as the former slave, but once untied he remained placid, his gaze darting between us and our weapons, filled with disbelief and amazement. There was a brief moment of indecision, a calculation of whether to flee or stay. I tried communicating our mutual need for alliance, even resorting to his native language, but my words seemed to elude him. However, when the distant rustle of footsteps reached our ears, he gestured urgently for us to follow. His deteriorating health was plain to see; each breath sounded strained, and a worrying rumble accompanied his coughs.

"I suspect he has pneumonia, likely from a respiratory infection," Larissa remarked.

We sought cover near the imposing white tower, taking refuge behind a bus. Seeing the tower up close again after so long made my skin prickle with anxiety. Bodies, primarily women, were arranged seated against the wall. The bloodstains behind them spoke of their violent end. Beside the entrance stood another sign featuring the skull and the red line. A squad of masked soldiers marched past, their bayonets reflecting the nearby flames. As soon as they disappeared around a corner, we made a dash for the doorway.

A chilling breeze flowed through the hallway, bringing with it the stench of decay. Jacob activated his high-powered tactical flashlight, momentarily blinding in its intensity. The beam startled our Neanderthal companion; he recoiled as if witnessing magic, letting out a sound of awe before a spasm of coughs forced him to double over. He leaned against the wall, gasping. I couldn't fathom his perceptions of us. Trusting us, alien beings appearing out of nowhere with superior technology, would require immense courage, or perhaps sheer desperation. Initially, I assumed the tower was evacuated, but the source of the fetid stench soon exposed the horrifying truth. A large, windowless room had been repurposed into a ward, with each bed serving as the final resting place for a decaying body.

"This must've been set up at the onset of the epidemic," Larissa said. "Before they resorted to fire as treatment."

"Epidemic?" Jacob asked. "Is that what's unfolding here?"

I thought about the mine—about the harrowing fate they must have suffered down there.

"Look around," Larissa said. "These people aren't fighting a war, nor are they fighting any type of uprising… they're fighting a disease."

"And by the looks of it," I said, "they're losing."

Jacob's usually firm voice wavered, "Are we in danger of catching it?"

"It's too soon to say," Larissa said. "I need a secure location to examine the sick—one where we aren't constantly under threat from flamethrower-wielding soldiers."

We pressed on, guided by the soldier until he gave out, collapsing onto the floor in a coughing fit that left the concrete speckled with blood. We found ourselves near an elevator, sparking an idea I could only pray would work.

"This has escalated beyond simple reconnaissance," Jacob noted, casting his light over the fallen soldier. "We need to reassess our position and formulate a new plan before proceeding any further."

"I know a place," I said. "Last time I was here, they took me to a lab where they examined me. Larissa, it might have the tools you need. It was guarded then, but with all this chaos, it could be deserted. It's also the only place where I hope to either find Dura or at least get clues about where they took her."

Larissa eyed the soldier, then me. "How far is it? We have to carry him."

"This facility is a veritable labyrinth," I said, "but I believe I remember the way—"

Jacob cut in, "You believe? We can't navigate this on a hunch!"

I continued, trying to assure him, "This elevator leads to the garage. There might be a truck there we can steal. If so, all we'd need to do is locate an entry point to the underground route. My guess is the garage should have one. Though last time, they transported me and Alex there via a surface platform. So, I can't be certain."

Jacob frowned, thinking. "Why not just take the truck and return to camp? We could examine—"

"No," I said. "Once the soldiers report back, reinforcements will be sent, maybe even an airship. This might be our only chance to uncover the truth about this place... and perhaps to find Dura."

Jacob took a deep breath, "I hate to say this, but given what we've seen, especially with this epidemic, the odds of her being alive are slim."

"I need to at least try," I said. "And it's not just her. It's our child too. I can't just give up on mere probabilities." I paused, measuring his reaction. "If you want out—"

"It's not like that," Jacob said. "I'm with you. But I won't watch you die for a lost cause."

Larissa, sensing the tension, chimed in, "We should head to the lab. The camp is too far, and this man may not survive the journey."

As she spoke, the distant creak of the tower gates echoed through the hallway. Someone must have noticed our entry. The muffled sounds of gas-masked voices and hurried footsteps grew louder. We had been found, and capture was imminent. Jacob and Larissa hoisted the ailing soldier, practically dragging him into the elevator. I yanked the lever, and just as we descended, the masked soldiers burst into view, their guns blazing. For a second, we were pinned with our backs to the walls. Jacob returned fire, covering us as the elevator platform finally moved into the safety of the shaft. As we plunged deeper, the air grew stiflingly hot, and an acrid smell intensified.

"We can't stay down here for long," Larissa said, flicking drops of sweat off her forehead. "I'm concerned about these fumes. There's a coal mine beneath, right?"

I nodded, "Yeah, why?"

"I suspect it's on fire," she replied. "Such fires can burn for centuries, spewing toxic gases and reaching temperatures over nine hundred degrees. As far as we know, we might be traveling down a lethal cloud of carbon monoxide as we speak. This might be why the soldiers wear military-grade gas masks instead of lighter protection."

"They turned up the heat in Hell," I said. "Those poor slaves."

Upon reaching the garage, it was clear that Larissa had been right. Thick plumes of white smoke billowed from the vents, making the hot air even more suffocating. We needed to move—fast. Amidst the dim haze, only two cars emerged from the shadows, a fortunate sight considering I hadn't even dared to hope for one.

"Can you drive one of these?" Jacob asked.

"He'd better," Larissa said. "The elevator just went up again."

"I... I think I remember how Dura operated it," I replied.

Rushing to the nearest car, we positioned the ailing soldier in the back, while the rest of us squeezed into the front. As I scrutinized the dashboard, a flood of memories returned—everything but the crucial detail of igniting the engine. Anxiety gnawed at my insides as I fumbled with the switches and yanked at buttons, yielding no response.

"We're running out of time," Jacob snapped. "Come on!"

"Perhaps it's out of fuel," I suggested, desperately seeking answers. "I don't—"

The soldier in the backseat groaned, attempting to communicate.

"I think he wants to give it a shot," Larissa said. "Let him."

We shifted him to the driver's seat just as the elevator door slid open, revealing three armed soldiers who wasted no time opening fire. Jacob retaliated fiercely, sending them diving for cover, while Larissa and I jumped into the back seat.

"We need to move, now!" Jacob shouted, placing himself next to the Neanderthal. "Drive!"

Despite fresh blood seeping through the soldier's ear dressing, he seemed aware of our voices. He pushed down the steering wheel, a task nearly beyond his waning strength, and in doing so finally got the engine started. I tried to guide him on where to go, but was jolted back when he sped off. He made a quick turn, pressing us against the side, and then surged toward a tunnel I could only hope led to our destination.

"They've taken the other car," Larissa exclaimed, glancing back.

Sure enough, they were in pursuit. Our surroundings were blurred by thick smoke, tinted a ghostly green by the overhead emerald lights, and the angry engines filled the tunnel with insistent thunder. When the first gunshot rang out, it was almost drowned by the noise. Reacting instantly, Larissa and I ducked, just as a barrage of bullets shattered the rear window.

"Use this!" Jacob thrust a grenade into Larissa's hands. "Pull the pin, release the lever, count to two, then drop it in front of their car."

"Why can't you do it?" Larissa asked.

"You've got a better angle from back there!"

Larissa begrudgingly gripped the grenade.

"O-Oblonga!" I shouted, pressing my face into my knees. "Oblonga!"

"What's that supposed to mean?" Jacob asked.

"I'm not talking to you!" I snapped back. "I'm urging our Neanderthal driver to speed up!"

A deafening blast echoed behind us, making our driver swerve dangerously.

"I missed!" Larissa cried out. "It bounced to the side!"

"Don't toss it," Jacob instructed, handing her another grenade. "Just release it gently."

"I did!" Larissa shot back, her voice dripping with frustration.

I peeked above the car seat, trying to assess the situation. With her long hair repeatedly falling into her eyes, Larissa struggled with the grenade's pin, leaning perilously out of the shattered window. A soldier from the pursuing car thrust himself outward, firing rapidly. Bullets whistled through the air, a few kicking up sparks next to Larissa, yet she remained undeterred.

"Sharp turn ahead!" Jacob warned. "Hold on tight!"

Larissa slid sideways, almost tumbling off the trunk, and then—as soon as we straightened out again—she finally let go of the grenade. The explosion erupted right before the pursuers' car. For a fleeting moment, victory seemed ours, but they emerged from the smoke unscathed.

"You're hurt!" I noticed as Larissa settled back.

She grimaced, revealing a bleeding arm. "Shrapnel," she muttered. "Stings like hell, but I'll manage." Frustrated, she added, turning to Jacob, "I would've nailed them if not for that turn!"

Jacob gave her a reassuring look. "You did great. Third time's a charm!" He handed her another grenade, then shot me a sharp glance. "Cover her, Abasi! Don't just watch."

Taking a steadying breath, I readied my rifle and turned around. Our pursuers zigzagged to evade us, remaining elusive targets. As beads of sweat slid down my temple, my attention fixed on their gunner, now in the midst of reloading. Seeing Larissa brace herself, I knew it was my moment. My rifle spat out a stream of bullets, its recoil catching me off guard. I feared a misfire, but when I let go of the trigger, the soldier dangled limply from the other vehicle.

"Get down!" Larissa yelled, pulling me out of the surreal sensation of having killed.

I dropped just as a jagged car fragment hurtled through our back window, blasting past where I had just been, before lodging in the seat in front of me.

"Nice one!" Jacob called out. "You got them good!"

"I landed it right on their hood," Larissa replied. "I saw them slam the brakes and spin, but they were already done for."

Adrenaline surged through my veins, igniting tremors as a persistent ringing echoed in my ears. In the midst of this sensory onslaught, a numbness seized my mind, blurring my vision and distancing me from the surrounding chaos.

"Hey, Abasi!" Jacob shouted.

He had been trying to get my attention, but I hadn't registered it. I blinked, refocusing. "What?"

"Did you get shellshocked there for a moment?" he smirked. "Listen, can you tell where we're going? I mean, are we going back to the surface or what? We won't survive for long down here."

"I think this is the access route to the tunnel I mentioned—"

Before I could finish, the road dipped sharply, merging with the subterranean highway. The massive, corroded fans lining the road still turned, but rather than circulating fresh air, they now funneled thick smoke, which hung heavily in the tunnel, shrouding everything in darkness. The intense heat almost singed our throats with every breath, a discomfort made worse by the grim sight ahead. Bodies littered the road—predominantly Denisovans, but also some of their Neanderthal masters, their once-feared whips extending on the ground like lifeless serpents. Our driver, his complexion now eerily mirroring the pale corpses outside, cautiously navigated past them, taking care not to run over anyone. A solemn silence enveloped us as we witnessed the grim tableau, only to be shattered by the familiar roar of the underground waterfalls. Crossing the bridge that ran parallel to them, a welcome chill replaced the heat, and the promise of purer air became palpable.

"It's clearing up," Larissa said. "Can you feel it?"

"Are we nearing the surface?" Jacob asked.

"There's an underground river beneath us," I said. "It may have prevented the fire from spreading further."

A small figure sat at the bridge's midpoint, leaning against the ledge. We nearly passed by before I recognized who it was.

"Stop the car!" I shouted, jumping out as soon as we came to a halt. The mist thrown up from below clouded my vision, making it challenging to see, and I had to shout with all the power of my smoke-ravaged lungs to pierce the roaring water. "Sebast!" I called out, rushing toward the silhouette. "Is that really you?"

Like the others, he had turned pallid from illness. Still, upon seeing me, a smile crossed his lips, only for it to be interrupted by a cough so violent it threatened to shatter his ribcage.

I used the smattering of words I knew in his language to assure him I had returned to set things right. The top of his overalls was tied around his waist, exposing the scars of whippings on his bare torso. I extended a hand to help him stand. He shot a fearful glance at the soldier in the driver's seat, who met his gaze with apparent contempt, or at least a discernible revulsion toward Sebast's physical affliction. I opened the door to the back seat, gesturing for Sebast to sit between Larissa and me. Before settling next to him, I fixed the soldier with a meaningful look and spoke their term for friendship.

"Who's this?" Jacob inquired as we continued on our way.

"He helped Dura and me escape," I said. "It's a long story."

Upon reaching the road barrier, we stepped out of the car. The air was cooler than room temperature, and though the scent of fire lingered, smoke was nowhere in sight. Anticipating the presence of guards—either on duty or seeking refuge—I warned everyone to stay alert. Flickering lights from the garage's ceiling cast an unsettling glow as we approached the elevator, our every step imbued with dread. Yet, when we reached the floor above, it was clear the area had been deserted.

"This is where they held me captive," I shared, guiding them through the facility's desolate corridors. "I was a prisoner here for months. I must admit, it doesn't feel great to be back here."

Pausing outside my former cell, I peered through its observation window. Memories washed over me, vivid and haunting. I could almost see myself lying on the cold bed, gaunt and devoid of hope. Yet now, standing on this side of the glass, holding my submachine gun, a feeling of triumph stirred within me. The facility might have been empty upon our return, but it still felt as if I had come back as its vanquisher.

Larissa, supporting the now-feeble soldier, interrupted my thoughts. "You mentioned a laboratory. I'd like to examine my patients."

Leading her to the examination room, we found it in disarray, as if ransacked in haste. Overturned instruments, papers and shattered glass littered the white concrete floor, but much of the equipment remained intact.

As Larissa prepared, I helped the Neanderthals onto the examination table and took a moment to ask the soldier for his name. His eyes dropped to the floor briefly, then snapped back up to lock with mine.

"Koxa," he intoned.

Meanwhile, Jacob had settled in front of a desk, lifting a half-smoked cigar with interest. He brought it to his nose, taking a moment to inhale its scent deeply. "Surprisingly sweet," he remarked. "Nothing like the rich, earthy Cubans or Dominicans I'm used to back home."

Larissa carefully surveyed the room, assessing the array of unfamiliar instruments before her. With a discerning eye, she selected a few that bore a resemblance to the tools she was accustomed to in our world: an elongated device reminiscent of a stethoscope, slender fibered probes that could serve as swabs, and a peculiar viewing contraption she ingeniously adapted as an otoscope. To bridge the communication gap, Larissa demonstrated with her own actions, such as opening her mouth to show she needed to inspect theirs, seamlessly guiding the Neanderthals through the examination.

"Don't even think about trying that cigar," I warned, gesturing toward the Neanderthals. "You wouldn't want to contract whatever they're suffering from."

Jacob tucked the cigar away, took a deep breath, and looked me square in the eyes. "Gonna shoot you straight," he began, his expression serious. "This whole operation's gone sideways. We need to fall back, reassess. We were just supposed to be doing recon, damn it, and here we are, holed up deep underground with..." His eyes flitted to the Neanderthals, struggling to stay upright, then back to me, voice lowered, "...with a couple of goddamn Neanderthals."

"It might have been messy," I said, "but at least we've found people who can help us now."

"But they're dying." Jacob tapped his leg nervously as he spoke. "That tunnel could've been the end for us. And picking up this dwarf without consulting? Look," he raised a placating hand to forestall my reply, "we need to know what we're doing. Improvising is good within the framework of a plan, but planning within the framework of improvisation is deadly. All I'm suggesting is that we need a moment of pause, to deliberate our next move. In time, you'll get your payback."

"He might already have gotten it," Larissa chimed in.

I shot back, "What does that mean? This isn't about revenge. It's about saving my child—"

"Listen," Larissa said, "these folks seem to be battling a respiratory disease. While I lack the proper tools for a definitive diagnosis, it seems likely this pathogen is a new introduction here, given its prevalence. Considering their limited population and whatever containment efforts they may have tried, I'd say this has been spreading for just over a year. And it's more than a little suspicious that its emergence coincides with your last visit."

I swallowed hard. "Are you implying...?" I started, but my voice faltered. "But we weren't sick!"

"It's possible one or both of you were asymptomatic carriers," Larissa said. "It's not unheard of for individuals to carry and spread a disease without showing any symptoms themselves. These Neanderthals would've been completely vulnerable, having had no prior exposure to the pathogen and consequently, no built-up immunity. History gives us numerous examples of this. The catastrophic depopulation of indigenous populations during the European expansion is a glaring case in point. Think about it—diseases like smallpox, measles, and influenza, which were relatively common and often non-lethal among Europeans, decimated native populations who had no defense against them. It's a tragic pattern that's played out time and time again throughout human history."

My knees grew weak, realizing my potential role in this catastrophe. I braced myself against the wall, preventing a fall.

Larissa softened her tone, "Dura was young; she might've had a fighting chance."

"But aren't we at risk, too?" Jacob said. "We've never been exposed to their diseases."

"Not necessarily," Larissa began, pausing thoughtfully before diving into her explanation. "The dynamics of disease transmission between the Old World and the New World weren't symmetric. One of the key reasons is that Europe had been an agricultural society for millennia. This close contact with domesticated animals like cows, pigs, and chickens led to a number of zoonotic diseases—infections that jumped from animals to humans. These diseases, over time, became endemic in Europe, meaning they were constantly present at a baseline level, and many Europeans developed immunities to them." She continued, "In contrast, while the Indigenous peoples of the Americas had their own complex societies and domesticated animals, they didn't have the same extensive exposure to animals that often acted as reservoirs for major diseases. Therefore, they didn't have diseases like smallpox or measles to transmit back to the Europeans." She glanced at the Neanderthals as she spoke. "Now, consider the Neanderthals. While they might have had access to the same animals as ancient Europeans, given their smaller population size and the possibility they predominantly lived as hunter-gatherers without intense animal husbandry, their exposure to zoonotic diseases might have been limited. Hence, the likelihood of them harboring diseases that are novel and dangerous to us is relatively low."

"Both of you share roughly two percent of Neanderthal DNA," I mentioned, my weight still supported by the wall. "This could potentially offer some protection against their diseases. Though, I recall a study hinting that Neanderthal-inherited DNA increased susceptibility to the coronavirus during the 2020 outbreak."

"Why only the two of us?" Jacob asked. "Aren't we all in the same boat?"

"Not exactly," I responded. "Only those descended from populations who migrated out of Africa and mingled with Neanderthals possess that DNA. My lineage didn't intermix, keeping us purely Homo sapiens."

Jacob chuckled. "That's rich. I'll have to share that with the so-called 'pure Aryan' dimwits back home, trying to rope kids into their little clubs."

"At this moment," Larissa said, "our odds of dying from a bullet or suffocating in this place are significantly higher than catching an illness."

"I can't fathom that I might be the cause of all this," I murmured.

Jacob shot back, "They didn't exactly give you a choice when they nabbed you."

"There could be a way to help," Larissa said, "but it would necessitate a shift in our objectives."

My eyes widened. "You mean there might be a treatment?"

"It depends on the exact nature of their ailment," Larissa explained, drawing a breath to collect her thoughts. "We need to determine whether the root cause is viral, bacterial, or possibly even both. The signs are somewhat mixed—there's an ear infection, apparent sinusitis, and bronchitis, hinting at multiple infectious agents at play. Though the yellowish tinge of their mucus points toward a bacterial infection, it's not conclusive by itself. Additionally, the absence of a pronounced fever in both individuals is somewhat heartening—it suggests the body isn't battling a severe systemic infection."

"What difference does it make?" Jacob asked.

Larissa's tone was assertive. "A virus would leave us hamstrung without a vaccine. But a bacterial illness? That's where the potential of antibiotics shines through. And from my assessment, I don't believe a virus is the primary culprit. I suspect it's pneumonia causing most of the damage." She paused, ensuring she held our attention. "Now, I'm piecing this together from what I've seen, so it's not set in stone. But if bronchitis is progressing to pneumonia in these cases, antibiotics might be our saving grace."

With a doubtful expression, Jacob said, "If antibiotics were the solution, shouldn't they have fought this off by now? And where would we even find any? It's not like there's a pharmacy around the corner."

"I brought some," I said. "Not enough for this kind of undertaking, though."

"They may not have discovered antibiotics yet," Larissa said. "After all, penicillin was discovered by accident in the late twenties. Who knows how long it would have taken us to discover it if it weren't for Fleming's serendipitous mishap? It's the kind of discovery that could have happened years earlier or years later. Given the Neanderthals' apparent level of technology, their lack of a cure is indeed troubling. Still, I believe antibiotics are our best bet."

"Shouldn't we save the antibiotics we brought for ourselves?" Jacob said. "Like Abasi pointed out, we barely have enough to make a dent here."

"That's precisely why I mentioned a shift in our objectives," Larissa said. "We may need to produce our own antibiotics."

"You have the capability to do that?" I asked. "If it's possible, we should absolutely try. Sebast risked everything to aid me and Dura in the mine, likely saving us both. If there's even a chance to help him, I feel bound to try."

"In theory, I can," Larissa said, "but in practice, much depends on finding the right ingredients and having enough time. The equipment I've seen, like these glass containers, could be adapted for our needs, but they won't be sufficient by themselves."

"Look, I get it about your buddy," Jacob said, "but we had a plan: in, then out. The more time we burn here, the riskier it gets for all of us."

"Don't be shortsighted," Larissa said. "Successfully treating this disease could change everything, not just for these two but for their entire society."

"We can't save everyone!" Jacob snapped. "Once our mission's done, you can come back and—"

"Mission?" Larissa cut him off sharply. "Wake up! You're not in uniform anymore. The game's changed, and we have to roll with it. We, as in our species, unintentionally introduced this plague to their world, and I say it's our goddamned responsibility to do something about it if we can."

"Your ideals shouldn't blind your judgment." Jacob took a deep breath, his shoulders dropping slightly as he tried to find composure. "This guy, Sebast was it? Let's extract him back to base, administer the antibiotics we have on hand. We save who we can with what we have. Isn't that more reasonable?"

They turned to me, awaiting my stance.

"You're both right," I said. "I don't believe we should get sidetracked here, and not just because of my personal stake in this. My child is a hybrid, most likely made in the hopes of turning the tides in a drawn-out war—an introduction of DNA to their germline that might upset the natural balance here. I don't know enough about genetics to quantify the exact risk, but intuitively, preventing them from using a hybrid to infuse *Homo sapiens* traits into future generations seems like a good idea."

Jacob nodded, "That's what I'm—"

"However," I raised a hand to stop him, "the antibiotics might be a way for us to make friends along the way, which we need if we want to survive here long term."

Jacob exhaled slowly, casting a resigned glance at Larissa. "Alright, how long will you need?"

Larissa pondered for a moment. "The timeline largely depends on sourcing the necessary ingredients and the duration needed to cultivate and ferment the penicillin. Realistically, we might be looking at weeks to amass the dosages required for treatment."

Although we were likely already exposed to the pathogen, we quarantined Sebast and Koxa inside my former cell while Larissa concentrated on synthesizing the antibiotics. Assisting them with a wash in the lavatory—which, to my relief, still had a working water supply—I provided them with unused staff clothing and endeavored to create a more hospitable environment within the cell. After this, Koxa perked up a little, giving an impression of improvement. Yet, when I offered him water, his persistent coughing made it nearly impossible for him to swallow. Witnessing his struggle was heart-wrenching, and my hope for him seemed to fade with each painful cough. However, as I watched Larissa—a whirlwind of activity working tirelessly around the clock—my dwindling hope found a spark to reignite. Feeling a need to contribute in whatever way I could, even though I knew nothing about what she was doing, I asked in what way Jacob and I could assist her. She looked up from her work for a moment, her gaze intent. "I'll need you to find a number of ingredients," she said. Thinking for a moment, she continued, "To synthesize penicillin in these conditions we'll have to be innovative. The primary challenge is finding a source with traces of Penicillium chrysogenum, the specific mold that produces the antibiotic. Old citrus fruits or bread with blue-green mold could be a good starting point, but even then, it's a gamble."

"So, fruits and bread... Anything else?" I said.

"Wait." She quickly scribbled something on a piece of paper before handing it to me. It was a list, the ink smudged in places from her hurried writing. As I stared at it, she continued, "We need a good carbon source; sugar will suffice, though pure glucose would be better. It serves as food for the mold, allowing it to grow and produce the antibiotic."

Jacob grabbed the list from me and quickly looked it over. "Animal bones?"

"That's right," Larissa said. "They are crucial for extracting gelatin, which solidifies the medium we'll use for growing cultures. Then, as you can see, there's citric acid or lemon juice. It's not just for adjusting the pH—though that's vital—but some organic acids can also help in boosting the production of penicillin."

I pointed to another item. "Salt? And *distilled water*? That will be a challenge to—"

Larissa nodded. "Both are essential. Salt, in the right concentration, ensures a balanced environment for the mold. Too much can kill it; too little can lead to other harmful microbial growth. Distilled water ensures we're not introducing any other contaminants."

"And this?" Jacob inquired, pointing to the last item on the list.

"That," she said with a serious tone, "is perhaps the trickiest part. We need to find a place in this facility that's cool and dark, yet allows for some airflow—a place where the mold can grow undisturbed. Every single factor, from temperature to humidity, will affect our yield. So while you search for these ingredients, also keep an eye out for such a location."

As Larissa delved back into her work, Jacob and I explored the facility, searching for both the items on her list and any potential sustenance. Recalling the daily meals I had previously received here, I suspected a food storage nearby. Our exploration soon took us to it. It was a dimly lit pantry. As the door creaked open, the sight that met our eyes was a mix of hope and disgust. Wooden shelves were laden with an array of canned goods, sacks of grains, and sealed jars containing a variety of preserved items, all showing clear signs of age and neglect. Off to one side, a few rabbits hung upside down, their lifeless eyes attracting a swarm of flies.

Many of the food items were in an advanced state of decay. Although this was beneficial for Larissa's mold cultivation efforts, it posed a challenge for our immediate sustenance needs. As we sifted through the supplies, we discovered a few edible treasures amidst the spoilage: desiccated fish, vegetables marinated in a tart vinegar solution, a jar of honey, and a tightly sealed bag of dried fruits. It wasn't plentiful, but with careful rationing, it would buy us enough time to survive.

After thoroughly cleaning the pantry, its confined and humid environment proved to be a perfect breeding ground for Larissa's mold cultivation. With this key component settled, together with everything we found in the pantry, she had nearly everything she needed to proceed. Only two key elements remained to be procured: animal bones and distilled water. To source the former, Jacob and I carefully lowered one of the hanging rabbits onto a flat wooden surface, preparing ourselves for the delicate task of deboning. We pulled out our knives. I held the rabbit steady as Jacob made a careful incision along the back, skillfully peeling back the skin to expose the musculature underneath. Following the natural seams of the muscles, we carved out chunks of meat, ensuring they remained intact for potential meals. The bones, however, were our primary focus. We used the tips of our knives to disjoint the carcass, meticulously separating each bone without splintering them. It was a process Jacob had learned during his years as an avid outdoorsman, and although I was new to it his instructions was easy to follow.

The challenge of procuring distilled water was up next. In the lab, amidst the jumble of scattered equipment, we found glass flasks, rubber tubing, metal clamps, and an electric heater coil which we saw potential in repurposing as a Bunsen burner. With Larissa directing our moves, we jury-rigged a distillation apparatus. The process involved boiling water in a flask, allowing the steam to pass through the tubing, and then cooling it down. As the steam condensed, it dripped into a separate container, giving us a clear, distilled liquid free from impurities. The principle was simple, but the assembly required precision.

Now armed with the necessary bones and distilled water, Larissa was ready to embark on the next critical phase: the actual synthesis of the antibiotics.

While she worked on this, Jacob and I took on the mantle of caring for the sick. Our roles, though they felt overshadowed by Larissa's sophisticated endeavors, were vital: we ensured that Sebast, and more urgently, Koxa, stayed hydrated and as comfortable as their conditions permitted. As the days bled into one another, the stark reality of Koxa's deteriorating health became undeniable. At one point, the grim prospect of preparing for his imminent passing became a whispered, mournful topic between Jacob and me.

Yet, just in the nick of time, Larissa's relentless efforts bore fruit: she managed to complete her first batch of antibiotics just as Koxa's condition reached its critical point. Before administering the freshly cultivated treatment to him, she paused, her demeanor serious. "Dosing is a challenge," she warned. "This hasn't been refined in a proper lab setup, and we have no way of conducting standard dose tests. There could be side effects, and there's no guarantee of the strength of each dose."

Taking the risk, she cautiously started Koxa on a regimen, giving him approximately 125mg every eight hours. Within days, a transformation was evident. Koxa, who had teetered on the brink, began to rally. Sebast, his condition not as dire as Koxa's to begin with, showed signs of improvement even more rapidly.

I found Larissa in the examination room, seated on a stool amidst glass containers and makeshift Petri dishes. She was visibly weary, but her face bloomed with a smile of profound relief. I lingered in the doorway for a moment, taking it all in, before declaring, "You've done it. All your hard work has paid off."

She looked up and nodded gratefully. "Thank you. They should be back on their feet within a week."

Just then, Jacob walked in, concern etched on his face. "Our rations are almost gone," he began, glancing between Larissa and me. "If we're here for another week, hunger will really start to bite. I mean, we're already feeling it, but..." He trailed off, searching for words. "Any idea what conditions might be like topside by now?"

Larissa furrowed her brow, considering his words. "Do you think they're waiting for us to come out? The extermination process should be complete. If they're not waiting, they might've quarantined the entire area. Either way, I'd bet on guards being stationed at the exits."

"We need to be prepared for any scenario," I said. "Let's stay put for one more week. Once the Neanderthals are back on their feet, they can help us out."

Over the next week—the fourth since our arrival at the facility— I decided to involve Sebast in our planning. We had stumbled upon some maps in a drawer, and I was eager to show them to him, seeking any knowledge about Dura's potential location. He sifted through them until he landed on one of Europe. He pointed at a skull icon—presumably marking a settlement— placed close to what would have been Vilnius in our own world.

"That's a good hundred and fifty miles away!" Jacob exclaimed. "Is he certain she's there?"

"I can't say for sure," I admitted, "but he seems pretty confident." Turning to Sebast, I pointed at the presumed population center. "Dura?"

"Dura," Sebast affirmed.

"Could it just be the name of the settlement?" Larissa wondered.

"No," I clarified. "The text under the skull indicates something else. And I'm fairly certain he grasped my question about Dura. He knows who she is. They were familiar with each other."

"But how does he know they took her there?" Jacob pressed. "He was just a slave, wasn't he?"

I shrugged. "Perhaps it's an educated guess, based on the place's significance. Maybe it's a key settlement or even a capital. Regardless, it's the only lead we have."

As we deliberated, Sebast and Koxa fell into a heated exchange, with gestures toward us and then to themselves. While the crux of their dispute remained cryptic, Sebast's perspective seemed to prevail—hopefully to the benefit of our plans.

"We need to secure a bigger transport," Jacob asserted, refocusing the discussion. "If our base camp is still operational, we can use it to load up and haul everything out."

"Don't forget about this equipment," Larissa added, looking around the facility. "It's crucial for making antibiotics. Who knows if we'll encounter another place like this."

"There's no way for us to lug all this to the surface by ourselves," Jacob said. "Our only option is to secure that vehicle, return for all this, and then make our exit." He shook his head. "I've handled complex ops, but this situation? It's a whole different level of FUBAR."

"I'll stay behind and pack," Larissa offered. "Sebast can assist me. The rest of you can focus on securing the vehicle."

"Are you sure about splitting up?" I asked.

"I'll manage," Larissa assured us. "If anything happens to you guys—God forbid—I'll find my way back to camp with Sebast's help."

"What if something happens down here?" Jacob asked.

"We've been here nearly a month," Larissa retorted. "I think we can consider this place relatively safe."

Koxa steered us back to the surface. I tried conveying our plan to him, though gauging his understanding was difficult. His face betrayed nothing but a trace of nervous uncertainty. It was understandable—after all, he was aiding beings from another world about whom he knew almost nothing.

The sun hid behind a dense veil of clouds as heavy rain rattled against the coachwork. We drove carefully, constantly watching out for movements among the charred remnants of buildings. Though the rain had doused the fires, ghostly tendrils of smoke rose from the mass graves, marking the ashen landscape with the haunting aura of a world turned to scorched earth. Still, emerging from our subterranean hideout felt liberating, and as Koxa rolled down the windows, the air, though tinged with the scent of burnt debris, felt invigorating compared to the stale atmosphere below.

No greeting awaited us. The area appeared deserted. Yet, mindful of potential guards, we kept our distance from the main entrance. Several trucks were visible, but all were burned out husks. Our car eventually slowed to a halt, likely out of fuel, forcing us to trudge through the ashy mire. The relentless rain obscured our vision as thunder grumbled from above the forest canopy. I spotted three imposing figures in the distance, noses to the ground, scavenging. My hand tightened around the rifle's grip.

Jacob squinted, trying to make them out. "What on earth are those?"

The beasts lifted their heads, locking eyes with us.

"Dogs," I said, "or rather, the Neanderthals' unique breed of them. They must have been left behind. I'd wager they haven't had a decent meal in a while."

The dog that had assumed leadership of the pack bore down on us, its head dipped, ears flat, and incisors bared threateningly under its curled lip. Its packmates fell into a threatening formation behind it. Koxa patted my shoulder, muttered something, and then bolted out of sight.

"Where's he going?" Jacob asked, aiming at the advancing dogs.

"Let's head back to the car!" I shouted, already in motion. "Don't waste your shots!"

Jacob stumbled, slipping in the mud. Wheeling around, I extended a hand to him. All the while, the dogs closed in around us, growling menacingly. Jacob fired a warning shot, but it didn't faze them.

"It's them or us," he declared, leveling his rifle at the alpha. "I hate hurting animals—especially dogs."

I scanned for Koxa, hoping to spot him amidst the debris, but he was nowhere to be seen.

"Even if we drop two, the third will be on us," I said. "Where the hell did our friend go?"

The dogs took a few daring steps closer.

"I knew we couldn't trust—"

A loud crash interrupted Jacob as a bus—the same type I had ridden the previous year—burst through the remnants of a nearby building. It barreled toward us, horn blaring, headlights blazing. The dogs, startled, scampered off. I tried to leap aside but slipped, landing face-first in the mud. The bus skidded to a halt, stopping just inches from us. Through the splatter on my face, I saw Jacob, laughing. Catching my breath, I asked, "What's so funny?"

"Sometimes, I love being proven wrong," he grinned.

Behind the bus's wheel, Koxa peered down at us.

"You guys had a mud wrestling match?" Larissa said, her voice tinged with amusement, as we returned. "I'm almost done packing." After we recounted our run-in with the dogs and described the surface conditions, her expression sobered. "Maybe they thought we didn't make it out," she said, "or their attention's elsewhere."

"Think the disease spread beyond here?" I asked, lifting a wooden box of glass bottles.

"I fear it has," she replied. "Containing something like this is nearly impossible."

We transferred the equipment to the garage and stowed it in the bus. As I reached for the last box in the examination room, I paused, taking in the surroundings. I knew I would never return to this unsettling place that had been both my prison and sanctuary. The thought of leaving stirred a strange melancholy, even though I was genuinely relieved to go. Clutching the box, I headed back to the bus. Once inside, I pulled on one of the Neanderthal hoods and settled next to Koxa, while the others hunkered down in the rear. Our plan was for Koxa to negotiate past the potential guards without arousing suspicion. If that failed, we would resort to breaking through the gates, trying our best not to hurt anyone.

As we reached the surface, the storm persisted in its fury. Under my cape, my fingers rested on the AK-47, prepared for the worst. As we had anticipated, two guards were stationed at the entrance, their faces obscured by black face masks. One approached the driver's seat where Koxa sat. I couldn't catch their exchange, and unable to tell if things were going in our favor, I felt the guard's gaze linger on me as if trying to peer beneath my hood. A dog accompanied them, its barks punctuating the air—either alert to our motives or simply agitated by the thunder. Regardless, it set my teeth on edge and tightened my grip on the rifle.

The guard then retreated slightly, communicating into his radio, his raised hand signaling for us to wait. It wasn't reassuring. He shouted something to his counterpart. I readied myself for confrontation, ensuring my face remained hidden. The second guard entered their booth, lifting a mouthpiece to call someone. I could sense Koxa's growing unease as he watched him. The guard then returned the mouthpiece to its holder seemingly without receiving a reply, possibly saving us from being exposed. He jotted down something on a piece of paper and handed it to his partner, who gave it to us along with some face masks. Though his parting words sounded like wishes for good fortune, I couldn't let my guard down until we were safely on the dirt road.

Upon returning to camp, which fortunately remained undetected, we began the grueling process of moving everything to the bus. We had to shuttle between the midway chamber and the camp, and subsequently from the camp to the bus. This meant multiple treks through the cave and repeated ascents of the hill. All the while, the thunderstorm, which had engulfed the valley upon our arrival, unleashed its full fury upon us. This grievous exertion tested our very limits and at times seemed unendurable beneath the violent lightning, leaving us as drained as we were drenched.

"I'm going back in for the solar panel roll!" I shouted against the roar of thunder. "It's the last—"

"I'll handle it!" Jacob said. "You look beat. Help Larissa with that crate. Leave this to me."

It wasn't until I took a moment to rest inside the bus that the full weight of my exhaustion hit me. I was grateful for Jacob's intervention but also concerned that his tendency to play the hero could undermine our collective efforts. After Larissa and the Neanderthals finished loading the bus, she joined me—also worn out but in a way that made her look more alive instead of less so.

"I'm sure he's a good guy," she began after I voiced my reservations. "I see why you brought him—you trust him, and I get that. But as you hinted yourself, he tends to see danger as an opportunity to shine, not a risk to mitigate. That doesn't mean he's not valuable—he's already shown his worth. But let's keep an eye on him to make sure he doesn't do anything too reckless."

"For sure," I said, paused momentarily, and continued, "How are you holding up?"

"I'm fine." She smiled, shaking her head in disbelief. "Another world, huh? I still can't wrap my mind around that. It's an adventure of a lifetime. I'm genuinely glad you brought me here. Who wouldn't be? It's an opportunity to witness a world untouched by man. Yet, a part of me is terrified—understandable, I guess, given the circumstances—that this might be a one-way trip. It's true that as a medical volunteer in different conflict zones, you become weary of getting too close to people, so I'm sure this would have been a bigger issue for someone else. I mean, I don't think I would have come if I had a partner or child waiting for me at home. Still, I've..." She cast a glance down at her hands, still grubby from climbing the hill. "I've made connections along the way, formed relationships here and there. Then, of course, there's my family—my parents, and my siblings. If I die here, they won't get any closure. My disappearance will just be one of those unresolved mysteries. I would become an endless source of worry, a hope destined to never be fulfilled. And that *terrifies* me."

"Me, too," I said. "Back in that cell, completely at the mercy of my captors, I was convinced I would never see my family again. The thought of my parents and sisters never knowing what happened to me was unbearable. So, yeah, there's the dream of exploration, and then there's the nightmare. And by now I know about the latter way too well."

We chatted for some time until Larissa remarked, "Shouldn't Jacob be back by now?"

Just as I was about to share her concern, I spotted a silhouette in the rain. "Speak of the devil," I motioned toward the doors.

Jacob, with the roll of solar panels slung over his shoulder, made his way down the slope. "This is it," he said. "Time to move."

"Night's approaching," Larissa noted, standing up. "Let's hold off until it's dark. The cover of night might give us some protection."

Jacob settled near the driver's seat, rain still dripping from him. The violent winds shook the bus, rain pattering above. Sebast, curiously eyeing our gear, reached for a weapon.

"Hands off," Jacob cautioned. "Here, try this instead."

He popped open a can of soda from our supplies and handed it to Sebast. At the first sip, Sebast's eyes widened in awe. Laughing, Jacob tossed a can to Koxa as well.

"From Homo sapiens with love," he quipped, glancing my way. "Might've just opened up a whole new world for them."

Larissa interjected, "We need a plan for when we reach our destination. It's crucial. We don't know what awaits—military base, city, or something entirely different. Ideally, we should establish a camp nearby and offer medical help from there. Our Neanderthal companions can introduce us to those in need."

"Let's not go in guns blazing," Jacob said. "We need to recon properly this time, then make a call on our next move."

"I agree," I responded, "but remember, Sebast identified that location for us on the map. He might have a sense of where to proceed from there. If it seems safe upon arrival, I propose we let him take the lead."

Jacob nodded, albeit with a touch of hesitation.

"Alright, then," Larissa said. "Maybe we should get going."

I showed Koxa the map, pointing out our destination. He murmured something, which I took as affirmation, before firing up the engine. Apart from our headlights illuminating the road ahead, darkness enveloped us—more because of the dense clouds than the descending sun.

"How long till we get there?" Larissa asked as we merged onto the main road.

"If we maintain this speed and don't hit any roadblocks, we're looking at a couple of hours," Jacob estimated.

Contrary to Jacob's hopes, we did encounter an obstacle. While it was minor, its somber nature struck a chord with me. An imposing tank blocked our way, its grand white cannon accented with silver flourishes reminiscent of a 17th-century ship's bow. Gilded bear silhouettes adorned its sides, presenting a flamboyant departure from the Neanderthals' typically stark designs.

"Denisovans," I remarked, my eyes lighting up. "This has to be a Denisovan tank."

Larissa glanced at the obstruction. "How do we get it out of the way?"

Jacob added gravely, "Looks like there was a skirmish here. Stay sharp; there could still be troops lurking nearby."

Without a doubt, violence had unfolded here. Burn marks

around the turret hatch suggested a grenade had been thrown inside the tank.

We disembarked onto the road. The raging storm had mellowed into a soft drizzle, though distant thunder continued its haunting refrain. Bursts of light peppered the horizon, not born from the storm clouds, but something else entirely.

"They're fighting," I said quietly, my eyes fixated on the flashes. "Perhaps the disease has undermined the Neanderthals' defenses, tilting the war against them."

Larissa looked uneasy. "Is that where we're headed? Straight into a war zone?"

"Looks like the settlement's in their enemy's crosshairs," Jacob remarked, scanning the area. "Brief me on these Denisovans."

"Their name originates from Siberia's Denisova Cave, where they were first discovered," I began. "The cave was named after Denis, an eighteen century hermit who took residence there. Scientifically, our insights come mainly from DNA, given the sparse fossil evidence. My personal encounters have only been with enslaved Denisovans, so my grasp of their society is sketchy. But their culture, marked by opulence and ornamentation, definitely outshines the Neanderthals'."

Interrupting, Larissa pointed to some bushes beside the road. "If we clear this path, we can bypass the tank. I don't want to be stuck here any longer than necessary. This place isn't safe."

"Take the lead on that," I replied. "Get the Neanderthals to assist."

"What are you going to do?" Jacob asked.

"I'll look around and try to piece together what happened here."

"Don't go too far," Larissa said. "I don't want to come looking for you."

Approaching the tank, I swept my flashlight across the path.

Charred bodies littered the ground, so disfigured that discerning their species was impossible. Beyond the tank, in a small clearing, two more immobilized units lay in silence. From the scene before me, it was evident an ambush had taken place. Despite searching, I found no weapons; I suspected the someone might have seized them. With my flashlight clenched between my teeth, I clambered onto the nearest tank. Its interior was a blackened shell, home to two charred figures who seemed to have embraced in their final moments. I don't know what else I expected, but the sight left me disappointed. There was nothing but death to be found here. Sebast approached, and I assisted him onto the tank. Side by side, we looked out toward the distant battle. It was clear to me that, although we didn't speak each other's words, we were both feeling the same conflicting emotions I suppose every survivor is bound to feel among the dead: a mixture of confidence and apprehension, of invincibility and vulnerability. Surviving was, then as now, both a blessing and a curse.

Sebast pointed skyward. High above, a silent projectile streaked through the clouds, originating from the east and destined for the unsuspecting Neanderthals across the Great European Plain.

"Abasi!" Larissa's voice cut through the air. "We need to go."

As we neared our destination, the silhouette of a city, devoid of the familiar glow of electric lights, began to materialize. Towering, identical structures cast long shadows upon the banks of their version of the Neman River. The only building that stood out, even though it was just as obscure as the rest, was an enormous pyramid at the center of the city. Moving closer, we noticed a colossal concrete wall with evenly spaced guard posts encircling the city. Koxa steered us toward what appeared to be the primary entrance, located squarely on the city's southern border. Deviating now would be suspicious; we had reached a point of no return. I sat up front with Koxa, while the others remained hidden in the back.

The guards stationed at the imposing gate donned yellow masks—a clear sign that the disease had spread. We put on our own masks in response. Distant, trumpet-like sirens emanated from inside the walls, their sound echoing between the uniform buildings that now rose above us. Koxa presented a guard with the document he had received earlier. The guard briefly skimmed it and attempted to speak, only to be silenced by a bout of severe coughing. Defeated, he gestured for us to move on.

The city's main artery was a wide boulevard, dotted with tall streetlights that emitted a faint white glow onto the otherwise shadowy street, leading directly to the pyramid which towered above everything else like a colossal black diamond. From my vantage point, the only discernible feature on its façade were some large circular apertures at its midpoint. Below this imposing structure, only a sparse crowd of pedestrians wandered the streets, their faces obscured by masks.

I beckoned Sebast to guide us from here. He carefully approached the driver's seat and directed Koxa to make a left turn at the upcoming junction, diverting us onto a narrower street. As we drove on, our path was mostly clear. Only the occasional traffic lights, which shifted between blue and orange, posed brief halts. Koxa, ever vigilant, would stop at each orange hue, regardless of whether anyone was waiting to cross the street, likely playing it safe to avoid any suspicion. The sirens we had heard earlier waxed and waned in the distance and occasional coughs echoed from murky corners, but overall it was quiet—a silence that mirrored the monochromatic and monolithic character of the city.

We reached what appeared to be a less affluent district, characterized by smaller cubical buildings haphazardly stacked atop one another with no alleys between them. Throughout, the skull with a red streak beneath it was scrawled on walls, a symbol I now recognized as their equivalent of a plague cross.

Koxa's eyes darted nervously around the neighborhood. Sebast motioned for him to halt the bus, and after a brief, gesture-laden exchange with me, made it clear he wished for us to stay put. He then disembarked and vanished into one of the clustered buildings. I gathered that this district was where his kin resided and, by extension, the birthplace of Dura. The realization instilled in me a newfound sense of hope. Nevertheless, I couldn't shake the feeling that our greatest challenges still lay ahead.

"Is this our stop?" Jacob inquired, shifting restlessly at the back of the bus. "My legs are begging for a stretch!" Without waiting for my reply, he strode toward the driver's seat. "I peeked outside," he continued, "and boy are these people thrifty with their aesthetics. I mean, the entire city looks like an oversized graveyard!"

"It might look that way to us," I said, "but consider the Neanderthals' larger eyes. They probably have better low-light vision, which could make their surroundings appear brighter to them than to us. Or maybe it's a deliberate blackout to keep the city concealed from aerial threats. Though if that were the goal, the streetlights would likely be off too." I pondered for a moment. "But sure, I'm not denying their architecture has a certain dystopian flair to it. Still, I find their culture fascinating. They're so similar to us, yet utterly different. For instance, have you noticed the complete absence of flashy billboards? That alone speaks to a very different economic model. And the pyramid at the center…"

"What about it?" asked Larissa, joining us up front.

"It's the telltale sign this city wasn't built in our world."

Just then, Sebast reappeared, accompanied by an older woman whose head and chest were shrouded in a veil. As we stepped off the bus to greet her, she locked eyes with me briefly, then shifted her gaze to Sebast—her expression more puzzled than fearful. With a reassuring touch on her hand, Sebast began to speak softly, likely aiming to allay her worries and build trust. She cast a quick glance at Koxa, perhaps seeking validation of Sebast's words. After a moment's exchange, she nodded and gestured for us to follow her inside.

Dim lights overhead cast a faint glow over the narrow hallways, where the air was thick with the stench of suffering. Coughs echoed behind nearly every door, mingling with infant cries and the occasional distant boom of battle beyond the city walls. A young woman, her face ghostly pale, emerged from a room. She entered a communal bathroom—the standard here, it seemed—and coughed so hard she retched onto the floor. The elder woman led us to a one-room apartment with an adjoining pantry. The disheveled, unoccupied bed seemed like a sad testament to a missing or perhaps deceased resident. Aside from the bed, the room's only other furnishing was a wall-mounted chest of drawers. The absence of windows intensified the room's chilly darkness.

After leaving briefly, the woman returned with a group of young men. Their joyful reunion with Sebast was clear, though their gazes toward us were riddled with suspicion. Even Koxa's presence seemed to surprise them. As they engaged in intense conversation, more faces—both young and old—peeked in, their curiosity unmistakable. The older woman, who appeared to command some authority here, signaled for them to keep their distance.

"What's the chatter?" Jacob asked. "We're boxed in here. Doesn't feel very safe."

Larissa's eyes, filled with compassion, stayed on the ailing residents. "I hope they're explaining the treatment. We need to bring in my equipment; I want to begin helping as soon as we can."

"Agreed," Jacob said. "But let's stash the rest of our gear somewhere else for now."

I quickly relayed our plans to Sebast, who in turn shared them with the older woman. Almost immediately, the young men dispersed, beginning to unload the bus.

"No, not the weapons!" Jacob barked. "Can't they just unload the glass bottles and—"

"Let's just move everything indoors first," I said, retrieving a box from one of the men. "The bus needs to be relocated. It stands out here and might attract the wrong kind of attention."

Jacob nodded in agreement. With a shared sense of urgency, we spent the remainder of the night ferrying our supplies inside and arranging them. Meanwhile, Sebast was able to convince the older woman to secure an additional room where we could safely store our arsenal. With that settled, as dawn approached, Koxa took the initiative to relocate the bus to a less conspicuous spot. Soon after, fatigue set in. Using folded military blankets as makeshift pillows, we attempted to rest, but the palpable despair around us made sleep elusive.

"We should administer the antibiotics to a couple of their most ill," Larissa said. "It'll demonstrate our intentions and might earn their trust."

Jacob, eyes heavy with thought, replied, "We can't cure everyone. Will they get that? And if they do, will they accept it?"

"We don't have to treat everyone," I said. "Just enough to prove what can be done."

When we finally rose, Larissa gathered the antibiotics we had brought from our world to give it to the woman we had seen vomiting the previous night. Meanwhile, Jacob and I sought the older woman, wanting her to witness our gesture of goodwill. We found her in a bigger room—a kind of shared parlor—where the women in charge were having a meeting around a large stone table. Some were smoking with their masks dangling at their chins, forming a haze beneath the cold light above the table, and others were racked with coughs. The room fell silent as we entered, all eyes turning to watch our next move.

Sebast sat on a stool beside a chalkboard, attempting to sketch two circles symbolizing our respective worlds. I couldn't tell if he conveyed our origins in a way that made sense or if anyone believed him, even if he did. Koxa stood alongside, presumably sharing the grim story of their government's actions at the mine—a tale far easier to believe.

An assortment of our belongings lay spread on a table before them. They were either laid out by Sebast as proof of our claims or placed by the others for him to explain. Thankfully, they hadn't brought in any weapons, their purpose likely obvious. Instead, they had opted to display the items that likely appeared most alien to them: a few glow sticks, a laptop, and a drone.

Taking initiative, I approached the table.

"Wait," Jacob warned, catching my sleeve. "Don't show them—"

"We need to display our capabilities," I countered. "That should settle any doubts."

Shrugging off Jacob's grip, I grabbed the controller and the drone. I switched it on, set it on the table, and fired up the rotors. The sound, reminiscent of a swarm of bees, startled several in the room. When the drone lifted off, two women leapt to their feet, retreating to the wall. As I maneuvered the drone, the entire room watched in wide-eyed wonder until the battery, having not been charged in such a long time, quickly ran out, forcing me to bring the device back down.

"That should make an impression," I said, looking at their astonished faces. "Now, let's introduce them to the medicine."

Once the room's tension eased, we led them to where Larissa was preparing to administer the antibiotics to the young woman. Lying in bed, her complexion nearly as gray as her soiled sheets, the woman hesitantly took the pills under the watchful eyes of the gathered crowd. Sebast murmured comforting words to her.

Larissa turned to me, "Can you find out her name for me?"

I posed the question to the woman, who stuttered her name between coughs. It was Oind.

Larissa dedicated days to treating her and two other Neander-thals. Employing the advanced, factory-produced antibiotics we had brought, their recoveries were swift. As the health of Sebast's people improved, the unease and suspicion surrounding us began to fade. Larissa became a magnetic presence in their dimly lit corridors. Children frolicked near her as she walked, while adults, both men and women, sought her out—some to discuss their ailments, others to lend a helping hand. In grati-tude for our help, they reciprocated by enhancing our living conditions—meticulously cleaning our room, outfitting it with additional bedding, and even preparing meals. Although their fare barely surpassed what I received during my captivity, we remained deeply appreciative of their hospitality.

Once Oind regained her health, she fervently helped Larissa in setting up equipment to produce more penicillin. She stepped into the role of her assistant, and as they worked together, tirelessly around the clock, they even began to pick up pieces of each other's languages. Larissa, displaying an uncanny knack for linguistic assimilation, rapidly outpaced my own efforts to learn their tongue.

Similar to our earlier challenges at the underground facility, procuring the necessary ingredients was a hurdle. However, with more hands to assist, it wasn't as daunting as before. Gradually, Larissa transformed parts of the apartment and adjacent hallway into a makeshift penicillin lab.

Meanwhile, Jacob and I took on the task of strategically relocating our weapons and tactical gear to a rooftop hideout, housed within a cluster of wooden sheds. This served a dual purpose: to declutter our living space and to safeguard against potential loss by not keeping all our essential equipment in one place. We meticulously inspected each piece of gear before securely stowing it away. Following this, we spread out the solar panels to charge our devices under the sun's energy.

Surveying the city from our rooftop vantage point, we glimpsed it in daylight for the first time. Three imposing airships hovered above the pyramid, its peak peering above the surrounding architecture. I watched people meandering through the streets below, and despite all that had transpired, it still struck me as peculiar that these individuals, so immersed in their daily routines, were of a different hominid species than myself.

Sebast joined us and gestured toward the pyramid. "Dura," he articulated, followed by a sentence that eluded me.

Trying my best to phrase it in his language, I inquired if she was being held there.

He responded with their word for "yes."

While relief flooded me, it came hand in hand with frustration. Dura and our child were close, yet seemingly unreachable, ensconced within what was likely the most fortified stronghold in this unfamiliar world. However, my hope wasn't extinguished. I held onto a strong belief that Sebast's people would aid us in our rescue, not merely out of gratitude for our medical help but also for Dura's sake, their kin, and give us a fighting chance.

"Don't fret," Jacob assured me. "We'll extract them somehow."

As Larissa devoted herself to treating those most severely afflicted with the disease, Jacob and I finally began to plan the rescue mission in detail together with Sebast and some of the women in charge. As it turned out, they were indeed willing to assist us. Although unfamiliar with the pyramid's innards, they knew of its entrances and a seemingly connected sewer system. Navigating through language barriers, we reached a consensus: entering via the sewers with a small team, perhaps five individuals, while coordinating a diversion at the main entrances seemed the optimal strategy. In the subsequent weeks, they dispatched scouts to gather more intelligence. Each return brought valuable insights—details about entrances, exits, and guard schedules. Gradually, our nebulous notions transformed into a concrete plan of action.

Larissa, deeply engrossed in saving lives alongside Oind, chose to stay behind and continue her vital work. With the help from the Neanderthals, we didn't need her to risk her life—a life that, in the grand scheme of things, was more important than my own in this plagued world.

As she tirelessly treated the sick, tales of us and our miraculous cure spread among the city's impoverished residents. Drawn by these stories, families often arrived at the break of dawn or under the cover of night, bearing their sickest loved ones, pleading for our aid. Jacob voiced concerns over the potential dangers of this growing attention, but Larissa was resolute. She believed that by aiding these people, we would gain more good-will and trust among the masses. Driven by her innate sense of compassion and purpose, she took in the ailing, thus amassing a following with Oind emerging as her most devoted apprentice. The sight of Larissa's efforts was heartwarming. Yet, as Jacob had cautioned, it wasn't without its perils.

The day before our rescue operation, the usual knock of a family seeking aid was replaced by the heavy, foreboding thud of armored boots. Jacob and I were elsewhere in the building, unaware of the threat until the startling sound of a gunshot echoed through the hallways. Alarmed, we rushed toward the sound, eventually reaching the corridor leading to the entrance. Soldiers were ransacking rooms, tossing their contents into the hall, amidst which sat Larissa, kneeling beside Oind, crying and clutching her hands. It wasn't immediately clear to me, but Oind had been hit by the bullet. The hallway echoed with shouts as two soldiers held a group of residents at gunpoint, forcing them against a wall. A short distance away, the rest of the soldiers were confiscating Larissa's medical equipment, loading it into a vehicle that looked like a militarized semi-trailer. Amidst the turmoil, a formidable woman in a red uniform stood out, puffing on a cigar with unsettling calm.

"Stay back," Jacob whispered as I was about to intervene. "Don't get spotted."

We darted to the roof and peered down at the unfolding scene. Larissa was being escorted toward the truck. Panic gripped me. "What's the plan?"

Jacob was already in action, taping a grenade to our drone. "Can you maneuver this drone into the truck's cabin within four seconds?"

"I can try," I responded, heart pounding.

I revved up the drone, and the moment Jacob pulled the pin

and let go of the grenade's lever, I piloted the device toward the truck. A few soldiers shot at it, their bullets zipping past. Seeing the alien technology buzzing toward them, they scrambled for cover behind the truck with terror etched on their faces. The grenade's weight made the drone dip, forcing me to navigate it under the truck rather than into the cabin. Yet, it did the trick. The explosion rocked the street, blowing out nearby windows and sending shards of metal whizzing past us. Reacting instantly, soldiers rushed Larissa out of the trailer. The woman in red burst out of the building, her eyes shooting upward, locking onto our position.

"She spotted me!" I gasped, instinctively crouching. "That officer—"

"Use your rifle!" Jacob bellowed. "I'll mount the bigger one!"

With adrenaline surging, I raised my rifle and targeted the woman in red. The barrage from my gun sent everyone scattering again. Though I aimed for the officer's torso, my bullets found her leg, hobbling but not incapacitating her. A soldier dragged the officer behind the trailer just as a hail of gunfire erupted toward the roof. Meanwhile, two soldiers sprinted into the building, likely to pinpoint our location.

Koxa appeared beside us, rifle in hand, as Jacob emerged from the shed, lugging the massive machine gun into position.

"They're on their way up!" I warned. "We don't have much time!"

"Where's Larissa?" Jacob's eyes scanned the area below.

"They've taken her behind the trailer," I replied.

"How many are coming for us?"

"Two, maybe three," I said.

"You handle them," Jacob instructed, positioning himself behind the machine gun.

I spun around and hunkered down, my sights trained on

the entrance. Koxa stationed himself adjacent to the door. As Jacob unleashed a torrent of gunfire onto the street, the soldiers stormed onto the roof. They were hopelessly outmatched. I instantly took down the first one, while Koxa dispatched the other with a shot to the back.

"Great shot!" I yelled, despite knowing he couldn't understand.

Jacob, eyes intense with focus, called out, "I've suppressed most of them, but those behind the trailer are still a threat. We need to move before they regroup or receive reinforcements!"

Ditching the machine gun for his pistol, Jacob led the way to the stairs. I was on his heels. The building's residents hid in their rooms, yet Oind remained motionless on the floor, her life claimed by the bullet wound. Pausing momentarily by the exit, we formulated a quick plan. "I'll go left, you go right. On three," I said.

At three, we burst through the door, weapons ready. The woman in red limped into view, holding Larissa hostage with a blade to her neck. I locked eyes with Jacob; we were both awash with uncertainty.

"Let her go!" Jacob shouted futilely at the officer.

"Run!" Larissa's voice broke through, tears shining in her eyes. "Save yourself—"

"We're not leaving you!" I shouted. "I can't let them take you. You don't understand what they'll—"

"I do understand!" she said. "But they won't kill me."

A squad of soldiers stormed the street, their advance followed by a stark, imposing tank. The mechanical clink of its treads echoed as it aimed its barrel unflinchingly at us. Without warning, it fired. The hiss of the projectile split the air as it narrowly missed us, detonating against the building's exterior. Chunks of concrete and dust cascaded down upon us.

"Get out of here!" Larissa screamed. "Now!"

"We'll be back for you," Jacob vowed, gripping my dust-covered shoulder and yelling above the ringing in my ears. "We need to move!"

Scrambling over the rubble of the collapsed façade, I hastened after him, weaving through the building's corridors and ascending its stairs to the rooftop. Along the way, we found Sebast huddled under a table. Pulling him up, we continued our frantic ascent. Koxa, awaiting our return on the roof, approached us, evidently puzzled by the situation. I quickly explained that it was time to set our long-planned mission into motion. We didn't have enough time to assemble the team we had planned to use—the strongest men and women of their people—so we had to settle with us four. I passed my pistol to Sebast, and a cluster of grenades to Koxa, who still seemed to favor his own rifle. Meanwhile, Jacob shouldered the rocket launcher.

"They're coming," I said, hearing the distant echo of boots.

Jacob grabbed a grenade, his gaze fixated on our remaining arsenal. "We can't leave this behind," he declared. With a swift motion, he pulled the pin and placed the grenade amidst our stash of explosives. "Run!" he ordered.

Led by Sebast, the only one familiar with the path to our destination, we rushed down the stairwell. Midway, the explosion tore through the silence, its sheer force suggesting the building might collapse on us. Debris from the ceiling rained down on us, forcing us to dive for cover. Through the bedlam, Jacob's urgent shouts reached my ears, muffled and distant: "Move, move, move!"

As we continued on, my hearing gradually returned. Sebast directed us to a service room where he wrestled open a heavy iron hatch on the floor. A pungent odor, reminiscent of rotten eggs, wafted up. We braved the stench and descended into the abyss below. Once at the bottom, Jacob handed his flashlight to Sebast, who then illuminated a narrow corridor lined with moldy concrete walls and snaking copper pipes. The overpowering odor threatened to make me retch. Yet Sebast seemed unfazed, as though the putrid scent was a regular part of his life. I wondered if this foul place had once been his sanctuary or perhaps a secret passageway that granted him free movement within the city, prior to his enslavement in the mines. We hastened forward, our path intermittently crossed by darting rats, until we reached an opening that led to a larger, sewage-filled circular tunnel. A frail wooden plank offered a precarious bridge to a ledge on the opposite side. It creaked alarmingly as Sebast sprinted across.

"You hear that?" Jacob whispered. "Footsteps."

Realizing we were being pursued—likely by enemy reinforcements—I urged, "We need to move. Fast."

As the last one to cross the plank, the echo of the approaching footsteps heightened my senses. The plank groaned beneath me, dangerously close to breaking point. I paused momentarily, keenly aware that it might snap with one more step, then leaped toward the safety of the ledge. My hands clutched the rough concrete, feet sinking into the rank wastewater. The foul smell overwhelmed me, seeping into my lungs with every gasp of fear-laden breath. Scrambling to safety, I watched Jacob dispatch the plank into the water, eliminating our pursuers' means of crossing. As I hauled myself onto the ledge, a soldier appeared at the opening. Sebast promptly blinded him with the flashlight, providing Koxa with the perfect opportunity to deliver a lethal shot between his eyes. The soldier plummeted into the water and was swept away, but no sooner had he disappeared than two more soldiers took his place.

We sprinted along the slippery ledge under a hail of bullets. As they whistled past us, I instinctively hunkered down, arms draped over my head, struggling to maintain balance on the narrow walkway. When I dared look up again, Koxa had vanished. He had been shot in the back, the current instantly whisking him away. Despite the lack of time for thought or emotion, a sharp pang of regret pierced me. The poor man only scarcely understood the cause he had given his life for, yet his resolve had been unwavering to the end. *Could I honestly say I would have done the same in his place?* The lack of a clear answer filled me with a poignant sense of sorrow.

The soldiers turned around as soon as we got far enough away from them—perhaps to find another way—and it wasn't until several minutes later that we felt safe enough to slow down and assess the situation.

"This is far from a cakewalk," Jacob said as we entered a tighter tunnel with jagged rock walls and slightly fresher air. "We've lost our element of surprise. They'll be on full alert, weapons hot. We're in a real tight spot, no two ways about it."

"We can't stop now," I said. "Yes, they might anticipate us, but they're likely under orders to take us alive. That could work in our favor. Besides, they're currently grappling with both a war and a plague; they've got their hands full. Perhaps I'm clutching at straws here, but weighing everything, we might have a few advantages."

"They might need us breathing, but they won't think twice about dropping Sebast," Jacob said. "Koxa's already down."

"I'm painfully aware," I said, profound guilt weighing on my chest. "It's ironic. These people support us because we saved them. Yet Alexander and I... we inadvertently unleashed this plague upon them. If they ever found out, how would they look at us? I'm hardly the hero they believe me to be."

Jacob huffed a short, humorless laugh. "Guess they'd be pissed, but don't kid yourself, they'd do the same in a heartbeat if the boot was on the other foot. In this game, what separates the oppressed from the oppressor, the innocent from the guilty, the hero from the villain, it's all down to luck. That's one thing I've learned from war."

"Do you feel that?" I said, stopping in my tracks. "The ground is shaking."

"It sounds like—" Jacob began, only to be cut off when Sebast wrenched open a large metal door embedded in the damp bedrock. On the other side, a black train with blinding white headlights barreled past. The cars were filled with what appeared to be civilians, their faces barely discernible through the orange-tinted windows. A young boy pressed his face against the glass, his gaze meeting ours. When the train had passed, Jacob continued, "...a subway," his eyes wide with realization. "It is a goddamn subway!"

The striking convergence of technological evolution between our worlds left me awestruck, but it was the nuanced differences in our parallel innovations that truly captivated me. Though the train operated on familiar principles of locomotion, it was still obvious that it came from another world. It wasn't just the surprising integration of a suspension railway underground or the tubular train cars—it was also the aesthetics, the sleek obsidian finish and the vibrant orange windows. The juxtaposition of the familiar with the unfamiliar was, as often in this world, striking.

Once the train had disappeared from view, Sebast immediately darted into the tunnel beneath the suspended tracks. We followed close on his heels. Minutes later, we arrived at a station, a sprawling hall designed to resemble a natural cavern. Oversized orange lamps dangled from above, casting a warm, ethereal glow on the hall below. We edged closer to the platform, crouching low to remain undetected, yet I still managed to steal a peek at the waiting passengers, their forms mere silhouettes in the tangerine gloom. Among them were a man with a stroller, a woman puffing on a cigar while engrossed in what appeared to be a magazine, and two little girls engaged in a playful chase. The scene seemed utterly mundane, with no signs of danger, until I saw a group of soldiers patrolling the platform—no doubt in search of us.

As we reached the tunnel on the opposite side, we broke into another sprint. At every rail switch, the tunnel forked, causing Sebast to halt and evaluate our next move. I held my breath each time, but he always seemed to figure it out. Then, in the middle of an unusually long tunnel, a high-pitched hum began echoing from the tracks above, quickly followed by the blinding beams of another oncoming train. The tunnel left no room to sidestep, and the train closed in too fast to outrun. With swift, practiced movements, Sebast hurled himself flat on the ground. The train's trumpeting horn blasted, resonating in my chest as I too hit the ground, tasting the sharp, metallic bite of rail dust. In the stark glare, the space between the speeding train and the tunnel floor seemed impossibly tight. Jacob, reduced to a silhouette against the harsh glow, struggled to get the rocket launcher off his back. I held my breath, fearing there wasn't enough time, but just as the train was about to hit him, he executed a last-minute nosedive to the ground. As the train thundered overhead, the tracks above hissed with intensity. I could sense the train cars grazing my back, each a mere inch away from crushing me.

"That was too close for comfort," Jacob muttered as the train receded into the distance.

"We have to assume the driver will report what they saw," I said. "We need to keep moving."

Echoing my urgency, Sebast shouted for us to press on, likely having reached the same conclusion as me.

Despite the biting cold gusts flowing through the tunnels, sweat clung to my skin beneath my tactical gear. My muscles screamed in protest, urging me to stop, but the thought of Dura, our unborn child, and what would happen to Larissa if we failed kept me going. Pushing through the exhaustion that weighed down each step, I marched on, determination propelling me onward.

Sebast halted just shy of entering another station. While it bore similarities to the one we had just left, this one was distinguished by a grand staircase at the platform's end and an eerie absence of civilians. The only people here were a phalanx of soldiers standing guard near the stairs. A train hurtled by, not stopping for disembarkations. I pondered if the station was closed specifically for our manhunt or if this was its usual state of operations. Amidst the soldiers were a pair of massive beasts, tethered by thick chains that clanked against the floor and their jaws restrained by metallic muzzles.

"Are those dogs?" Jacob whispered.

The animals shifted erratically, their uncanny laughter reverberating across the platform.

"N-no," I stammered, swallowing hard, "they're not."

"Then what the hell are they?"

"Back home, those things are ancient history," I said. "Unless my eyes deceive me, we're looking at cave hyenas."

Jacob's reply was dry. "That doesn't exactly inspire confidence. What's our move?"

"I'd strongly advise against tangling with them," I said. "These creatures used to hunt wolves and even bears. Some theories suggest their large numbers in Siberia might've delayed humans from discovering the New World. Neanderthals had to vie with them for shelter and food."

Sebast gestured toward the soldiers, or possibly the stairs behind them, and whispered something.

"The entrance to the pyramid?" I mumbled. Turning to Jacob, I continued, "I bet the so-called sewer tunnel on the map they showed us was this station. Might be our only underground way in."

Faint radio chatter echoed from behind, growing louder, accompanied by the unmistakable sound of boots against stone. Soon after, the probing beams of flashlights began to paint the walls further down the tunnel system. We were running out of time.

With an urgent swiftness, Jacob readied his rocket launcher. "Bet they won't be expecting an RPG-7," he snarled. "Get to the center of the platform and lay down some cover."

Sebast and I slinked alongside the platform as the hyenas' agitation swelled. It was as though they sensed the impending turmoil, their unnerving laughter escalating to a near hysterical pitch. At the end of the platform, Jacob began his climb, while Sebast, unable to mount the raised structure, veered toward a ladder at its terminus. Finding myself in the middle, I double-checked my rifle, ensuring a round was chambered, and opened fire on the soldiers. In the ensuing chaos, they zeroed in on me, leaving Jacob unnoticed.

The rocket hurtled across the platform, detonating with an explosive fury that sent a wave of heat my way. Sebast was already on the platform, weapon in hand, shooting into the fiery aftermath. I climbed up to join him and quickly neutralized two soldiers who had miraculously survived the explosion.

A squad of five more soldiers stampeded down the staircase. I timed my grenade throw perfectly, lobbing it just as they reached the foot of the stairs. Trusting Sebast to handle any survivors from the blast, I shifted my focus to Jacob. One hyena lay motionless at his feet, but the other was locked onto his arm, gnashing and tearing.

"Get this damned beast off me!" Jacob gritted out. "Get it off, now!"

Instinctively, I pulled my rifle's trigger, expecting the familiar recoil. But only silence ensued. One glance at the empty chamber and I knew—I was out of ammo.

"Shoot the bastard already!" Jacob grunted.

"I can't," I said. Desperate, I aimed a powerful kick at the beast, but it held fast. "I'm empty!"

Grimacing in pain, Jacob nodded toward an extra magazine in his pouch. With shaking hands, I ejected the spent clip, slammed in the new one, and chambered a round. As the bone in Jacob's arm gave an agonizing crack, I took aim and pulled the trigger just as the hyena lunged for his face. It yelped, scampered a few feet, and collapsed. By now, the reinforcements from the tunnels had caught up to us. I laid down cover fire as I helped Jacob to his feet. Despite his injured arm, he managed to pull the pin on his last grenade and lob it toward the oncoming soldiers. With the explosion as our cover, we dashed to the entrance, finding Sebast standing atop a pile of bodies, his face etched with shock. I crouched next to him, quickly ensuring he was unharmed. Meanwhile, more soldiers had regrouped and were now rushing toward us from the platform's far end. As we made our way up the stairs, still underground, a sprawling elevator hall unveiled itself. The distinctive clang of metal echoing from the shafts indicated descending platforms—likely carrying reinforcements. Behind, the soldiers were hot on our trail, reaching the stairs. Time was rapidly slipping through our fingers. I looked to Sebast for guidance, but he appeared just as uncertain as Jacob and me. Even for him, this was unknown territory. One of the elevators reached us before the rest, revealing a trio of guards. We reacted instantly, downing them before they could react. As we piled into the elevator, a hail of bullets from the soldiers trailing us tore through the air. In haste, I jammed the lever to an arbitrary floor. The platform began to ascend, barely missing a lunging soldier's outstretched hand. We barely had time for a sigh of relief before Sebast slumped to the ground. I fell beside him, trying to gauge the severity of his wound.

"He's hit," I choked out. "They got him."

I began tearing at his clothing, desperate to see the wound, to try and stem the tide of blood.

"There's no time," Jacob said, his voice breaking from its usual hardness. "There's nothing we can do."

"No!" I protested. "We can't—"

Sebast grasped my hand, his grip halting my futile efforts. The guilt that welled up as our eyes locked was a torrent, and my tears flowed as much from sorrow as from remorse. He traced the path of my tears with a feeble touch, yet his own eyes remained dry. Instead, he mustered a smile. His eyes held a silent conversation, a wealth of unsaid words we would never exchange, only to close shortly after. And just like that, he was gone. As the elevator came to a halt, we had no choice but to run, leaving him alone on the cold, unfeeling platform.

We burst into an expansive corridor. It curved in a perfect circle around the heart of the pyramid. Along the inner wall, a series of imposing doors echoed an identical sound, hinting at a shared space beyond them. Surprisingly, for a society as stern as this one, it was the sound of music—the first I had ever encountered in this world.

We cautiously opened one of the doors. A potent mix of marijuana and incense wafted into the corridor. Beyond the threshold lay a chamber reminiscent of an indoor colosseum, with the entrance we used positioned at the top of the seating tiers. The source of the singing wasn't the stage but the red-clad women watching it. Their bodies swayed rhythmically as they lent their voices to an ethereal melody that was a strange fusion of sacred hymns and a heartrending opera. At the stage's center, atop a stone altar, a large woman of middle years straddled a young man not much older than Dura had been when she was forced into my cell.

"Are they—" Jacob said, as we made our way down the seating, having no other options.

"It's a mating ritual," I said. "This society is quite voyeuristic. I found that out the hard way."

While not all the seats were filled, a considerable throng still clustered around the mating pair. The occasional cough rang out, a grim reminder that even within these fortified walls, the plague had found a way in. Those nearest us noticed our presence, their expressions turning anxious as they whispered among themselves. Their unease spread, sparking a wave of confusion that swept through the hall. Then, the soldiers burst through the upper door, their gunfire slicing through the still air and sparking chaos. As the crowd scattered in terror, we found ourselves shielded in the ensuing panic.

We sprinted across the elliptical stage. The ample woman rolled off the young boy, plummeting to the floor before scrambling behind the altar for shelter. More soldiers entered from another doorway above, their shots churning up clouds from the marble stage. We veered toward a gate, presumably the stage entrance, and dashed down a staircase. A woman carrying an armful of clothes was coming up, her eyes widening in surprise. We brushed past her, pushing her aside. Her shout of indignation quickly turned into a pointed accusation as the soldiers appeared, her finger pointing our way. In the dim space beneath the stage, a few feeble yellow lamps barely pushed back the darkness. We proceeded with caution, quieting our steps. This area was cluttered with rows of costumes, forming an intricate maze, and large mirrors were dispersed throughout. The air was dense with a blend of overpowering perfumes, stale cigar smoke, and pervasive sweat. We used the clothing racks for cover, crouching low and advancing cautiously. The reflection in the mirrors showed soldiers entering the room. A hushed exchange of words, the click of radios being switched off, and the silent language of hand signals prefaced their division into two squads.

Every noise I made seemed amplified, every breath and footstep impossibly loud. Amongst the sprawl of the dressing room, a stage apparatus stood out, dotted with grimy gears and levers. Jacob signaled toward it, suggesting it as a hiding place. Then, a gunshot echoed. I froze. A mirror, reflecting my image to our pursuers, shattered. Someone shouted, sparking a hailstorm of bullets our way. Jacob returned fire, shredding fabric and ricocheting bullets off the concrete floor, as we took cover behind the apparatus. He then whipped around to face me, his shout piercing the chaos;

"We've got to leg it, or we're finished!"

I took a split second to close my eyes, attempting to center myself without success, then nodded. We sprinted, straight as an arrow, with the machinery at our backs. Risking a glance over my shoulder, I spotted the soldiers. They moved like shadows between the aisles of clothing, tracking us with predatory intent. Our escape route presented itself as an exit leading to a set of elevators. Jacob took up a defensive position at the door, fending off our pursuers with his remaining ammo while I frantically summoned an elevator.

"Jacob, it's coming!" I called as the platform approached our floor.

He thrust the rocket launcher into my hands as we stood braced to step onto it.

"I can't handle this with my arm busted up," he said. "We're out of extra rockets, so it's crucial that you nail the aim. Make this shot count!"

I gripped the launcher, feeling its weight on my shoulder. "I've got this." The echoing war cries of the charging soldiers filled the air as the elevator finally arrived with a metallic thud. I backed onto its platform, cocking the hammer and squeezing the trigger as I did so. Jacob shielded his head with his uninjured arm and dove into the elevator, narrowly avoiding the burst of flames trailing the rocket. I yanked the lever to send us down a floor, and just as the platform was about to descend, the concussion wave from the detonation among the soldiers knocked me off my feet.

"You gave 'em hell!" Jacob exclaimed, extending a hand to help me up. "That was a damn fine shot."

I mustered a smile, taking a grim satisfaction in the carnage I had wrought upon our foes. Yet, when I pondered on our odds of making it any further, a wave of despair threatened to engulf me.

"How on earth are we going to escape from this place?" I said. "We're smack in the heart of their society. It's daunting even to imagine how—"

"Shelve that thought," Jacob said. "Concentrate on the present."

His advice was sound, but my growing despair wasn't easily quelled.

Stepping out onto the floor below, we found ourselves in another grand hallway, this one bathed in a warm, salmon glow from massive lights hanging from the ceiling. It would have been an enchanting sight, if not marred by the surrounding despair. Protective masks, discarded tissues, and tattered linens littered the floor. Coughs echoed sporadically from a handful of rooms with doors ajar. A formidable female voice resonated through the public address system, cutting through the ambiance with its stark authority—undoubtedly alerting everyone to our intrusion. Even so, the onlookers—debilitated by sickness—barely registered our frenzied dash through the corridor. The imminent arrival of the soldiers had us on edge. We sought shelter in a nearby room, revealing an expansive apartment. Despite its larger dimensions compared to the dwellings in the impoverished neighborhood, its furnishings were equally stark. An elderly woman lay in bed, holding a white cloth bearing the evidence of her bloodied coughs as she pressed a hand against an inflamed ear. She tried to call out, but her sour throat stifled each effort.

Jacob's whisper cut through the silence, "Any ammo left? I'm dry."

I gestured to my last magazine and countered, "What about your Glock?"

"Lost it tangling with that damn cave hyena," he grumbled. "We need a game plan." He approached the door, pausing momentarily. "Wait." After pressing an ear to its surface, he added, "Soldiers are breaching rooms. We've got minutes, tops."

"Look at this uniform…" I trailed off, having discovered a wardrobe. My gaze flickered toward the pallid woman in the bed. "It's bold red with sleek accents. I suspect she's in a high-ranking position, maybe equivalent to a general."

"And your point is?" Jacob asked.

"It's a gamble," I said, "but we might be able to use her as leverage."

Jacob nodded, understanding dawning on his face. I snatched

the uniform and flung it at the bed, pointing my gun at the woman. "Put it on," I demanded, gesturing toward the attire. The frail woman clutched the duvet up to her chin, fear flashing in her weary eyes. "Put it on, now!" Though she didn't understand the words, the menace in my voice and the cold steel of my rifle made the message clear. With trembling hands, she began to dress.

"They're closing in," Jacob said, his attention riveted to the door. "We need to move, now!"

Taking swift action, I seized the woman and yanked her off her bed. As she fumbled with her uniform buttons, I nudged the icy muzzle of my rifle against her back, ushering her toward the door.

"Jacob, open the door and get behind me."

The sight of us holding the woman captive froze the soldiers. They barked out demands, possibly urging our surrender. The woman tried to assert herself, but her voice was raspy, hampered by continuous coughs that made her gasp for breath. As I maintained a firm grip on her shoulder, steering her backward, Jacob scoured our surroundings, frantically searching for an escape route.

"Stairs, over here," he called from a short distance further down the hallway. "Looks like they lead straight down to the entrance level."

Holding the woman close, I quickened our pace. Her racing pulse thrummed against my chin as I aligned my face with hers, aiming to present a smaller target. Her fear seeped through her sickly pallor, intensifying with each stride we took away from the soldiers. Upon reaching the stairwell, we broke into a run. Jacob hollered for me to drop the woman, but I suspected she might still be of value and dragged her along with a firm hold on her collar. Her hand shot out to clutch the banister, but I forced her to release it with a swift kick. The soldiers breached the stairs as we descended to the floor below, a mirror image of the one above.

"Where to now?" Jacob's voice rang out as he sprinted toward the elevators at the opposite end of the hallway. "We need a hideout, somewhere to think, because this game of chase can't go on forever!" Walking backward, I dragged the woman across the floor in front of me, keeping my rifle aimed at the door we had just come through. It wasn't until we had slipped into the elevator that I responded, "Our hostage might know a place."

"We can't trust her," Jacob said.

"True," I said, "but she's fearing for her life, and she might not want to risk it."

"How do you plan to talk to her? You don't know their lingo."

I shifted our hostage to face me, pressing the barrel of my gun beneath her chin. Our eyes met—hers hollow, mine intense. A single word escaped my lips, "Dura." The memory of leaving her behind in the biting cold clawed its way into my mind, igniting a fresh wave of guilt. "Dura," I insisted again, gesturing to the lever. "Take us to her. Dura!"

The woman's response was anything but clear. All she did was swallow hard and suppress a cough that expelled mucus from her large nostrils. After a moment that felt like forever, she gradually lifted her arm and guided the lever. As the elevator jolted upward, she faintly echoed, "Dura."

We placed ourselves behind the woman, using her as a shield. The elevator shuddered intermittently as it climbed. When it finally stopped, we cautiously stepped out onto the new floor. The hallway here was notably shorter than those below, suggesting we were approaching the pyramid's apex. No soldiers greeted us, but a few women in dark lab dresses emerged from rooms, retreating just as quickly when they spotted us. A slightly open door revealed what appeared to be a lecture hall, where a group of Neanderthals studied footage displayed on a projection screen. It showed the night of conception, the night I had finally given in to save Dura from perishing of thirst. Taken aback, I froze and stared at the screen, watching my then undernourished body leaning over Dura's as a fearsome shadow, my face twisted in agony.

"Is that—" Jacob began.

"Don't look at it," I said, filled with rage, and closed the door.

The rooms had windows here, tilted along the wall of the pyramid. They let in the gray light from the gloomy sky, and a heavy rain rattled against the glass. I called out Dura's name continuously as we pressed forward. Next, our hostage faltered, drained and unable to go on. She fell on her knees, crawled to the wall, and rested her back against it. I attempted to haul her back to her feet, but her strength had completely abandoned her. Absorbed in our predicament, we didn't even notice the elevator descending. When it returned, it brought up two soldiers. Jacob flattened himself against the wall, and in a swift motion, I dropped to a crouch, my rifle blazing. One soldier fell, but I was out of ammunition before I could deal with the other one. He ducked into a nearby room for cover. Glancing over, I saw Jacob on the floor, clutching his abdomen, pain etched across his face. The events had transpired so rapidly I hadn't seen what happened to him.

Kneeling beside him, I said, "You're not hit, are you?"

He gave a pained grimace. "They tagged me," his voice gruff but weak. Even with the force he applied to his wound, blood stubbornly spilled through.

Gathering my thoughts, I stammered, "We need to get you—"

He cut in, "Abasi, it's a no-go."

"What are you saying? We've got to get you to safety."

He coughed, "Got something to say. Listen up."

I strained to hoist him to his feet as the lone soldier cautiously advanced, murmuring into his radio.

"Stop," Jacob rasped. "Gotta tell you—" Blood seeped from the corner of his mouth. "Damn it, I'm sorry. Swear to me— don't let 'em take you."

His eyes fluttered, nearly fading, but then snapped back into focus. With an effort that seemed to take all he had left, he raised his arm, pointing past me. Turning, I expected reinforcements, but instead met the gaze of a young woman in a gray tunic. Dura.

"That's her, right?" Jacob said. His eyes met mine one last time before they closed. "I'm sorry, man."

"Don't apologize," I said, even though he was already gone. "If anyone should be sorry, it's me."

The soldier advanced, a quiver in his step. My eyes, blurred with tears, burned with contempt as I watched him. He was afraid, talking into his radio like his life depended on it. Dura sneaked up on me from behind, grabbed my wrist, and pulled me into an adjacent room. As the door swung shut, the soldier fired. A burning sensation grazed my neck, a too-close reminder of the bullet's proximity. Dura locked the door with fierce determination. Her emotions were inscrutable—*was she relieved to see me, or did she resent me for leaving her behind?* I gazed at her in disbelief, my eyes still filled with sorrow, but she barely glanced my way. It wasn't that she was avoiding me—at least not solely—she was intently searching for an escape.

I braced against the door, preventing the soldier's entry, but the room felt like a trap. Empty and without options. As minutes ticked away, a thought surfaced: maybe being captured wouldn't be so bad. Maybe they would imprison us together, granting us a chance to plot an escape.

My emotions were a tempest. I grappled with the grief of Jacob's loss while relief surged, knowing Dura was alive. I yearned to inquire about her well-being, our child's fate, and its whereabouts. Yet the urgency of the moment choked my questions. I had no choice but to suppress the turmoil inside me.

A glint in Dura's eyes diverted my attention just as another bullet pierced the door, narrowly missing me. Swiftly, she grabbed a chair, hoisting it above her head. Before I could even question her intent, she hurled it through the window. Glass shattered, and wind blasted into the room, sending papers from a desk swirling around. The soldier's boots thudded against the door, his voice raised in frantic shouts. From beyond the shattered window, an air-raid siren wailed over the city, its shrill tone reminiscent of a distorted saxophone. Despite the cacophony drowning out Dura's urgently raised voice, her message was clear.

Releasing my hold on the door, I sprinted toward her just as the soldier burst in. Dura was already making her escape through the smashed window. I seized her hand, my feet searching for purchase on the rain-slicked metal of the pyramid. Just as I began to find my balance, the soldier lunged, his hand fastening on my shoulder. My attempts to pry his grip were futile. I slammed my fist down on his hand, but his grasp remained ironclad.

"Get your damn hands off me!" I roared, drawing from a reservoir of adrenaline and landing a punch squarely on his face.

He let go, sending us hurtling down the pyramid's side with terrifying speed. A burning airship slowly spiraled from the skies, and skirmishes between Denisovan soldiers and their enemies played out on the streets below. The war had reached the city.

By sheer luck, I managed to grasp the edge of one of the massive openings in the pyramid's side, the sharp metal edges biting into my fingers. Dura was slipping past. I snagged her hair in desperation, halting her descent. The opening revealed itself to be a colossal vent, expelling a gust of warm air tinged with an unfamiliar, musty scent.

Dura climbed into the ductwork in haste and, reaching down, grabbed my hand—strands of her hair still tangled between my fingers. I murmured a thanks in her native tongue. I yearned to convey my remorse for our last parting, but in her language, I lacked the words. And even if I had known them, she seemed uninterested in revisiting that moment. She ran toward the first door she could find, not willing to lose a single second, and seemed frustrated by my attempts at catching up. I trailed behind, assuming she knew the layout. Our lack of weapons dimmed my hopes, but the ongoing war outside seemed to have thinned the ranks of our pursuers.

We stumbled into a darkened maintenance tunnel. Hot air blasted at intervals from overhead pipes, forcing us to proceed with caution. Clasping Dura's hand to keep from losing her in the darkness, we took a left turn. A faint light beckoned from the tunnel's end. Though we couldn't be certain, the sight spurred us to pick up our pace, hopeful it might be an exit. However, visibility was still scant, and within steps, we plummeted down a shaft, landing with a thud on a ventilation grill six feet below. My ankle twisted painfully on impact, a sensation worsened by my effort to suppress any noise. Dura, who had partially landed on me, appeared unscathed.

The space beneath us was bathed in a gentle purple glow. While our vantage only afforded a view of a portion of the floor, echoing voices and intermittent coughing suggested the room was vast. Climbing back up, especially given my injured ankle, was not an option. A screw tumbled from the grill, its clink on the floor sounding a chilling prelude. Within moments, our weight proved too much for the grill, sending us crashing down. Intense pain surged through me upon impact. With hands slick from blood, I strained to lift myself, managing to prop up on my elbows before the agony overwhelmed me. My vision blurred, yet I sensed Dura reacting to something. Shaking my head to clear my focus, I saw four guards aiming their guns at us. The room, awash in the violet hue, spanned the entire floor, its ceiling supported by towering columns. At its center stood a grand table, encircled by high-ranking women. Their collective gaze settled on us, a silent observation interrupted only by a few who succumbed to coughing fits.

Trapped, our options had run out. Dura tried to help me stand, but a guard quickly intervened, pushing her away to assist me himself. They led us from the room, and as we were ushered through the corridor, guilt and regret consumed me. Overwhelmed, I murmured apologies, haunted by the cascade of failures: Larissa's capture, the deaths of our Neanderthal friends, and the loss of Jacob. It had all been for naught.

When they tore Dura from my side, I screamed in defiance, but my efforts were in vain. They confined me in a dimly lit chamber beneath the pyramid—not a prison, but a storage room with a door too solid to breach. I speculated that perhaps the pyramid lacked designated detention areas and that the ongoing battle outside restricted them from relocating me, or perhaps that any existing cells were already occupied by prisoners of war.

The sounds of battle echoed through the walls, providing a constant backdrop to my confinement. For days, I clung to the distant gunfire, harboring hopes for a Denisovan victory despite my scant knowledge of them. As the days turned into a week, the din of battle gradually diminished. *Had the city been captured?*

Every time the door creaked open, I clung to the hope of seeing a Denisovan soldier, but it was always the familiar Neanderthal guards delivering my daily ration of poorly cooked meat. Though my ankle was starting to improve, I knew I wasn't fit for combat and dismissed the idea of overpowering my captors. My thoughts often drifted to Larissa. *What had they done to her?* The weight of guilt was unbearable. I found myself regretting not embarking on this perilous journey alone; it would have been harder, but at least my friends would have been safe.

Just as the confinement threatened to shatter my sanity, the guards yanked me from the room. The subdued overhead lamps stung my eyes, forcing me to squint. Before me stood two women clad in black, their batons casually resting in their hands. Though veils obscured most of their faces, the disdain in their eyes was unmistakable. I wondered if they blamed me for the plague. After all, those aware of my initial arrival should've been able to deduce my role in its onset. My mind raced: *Were they here to punish me?* But quickly, I surmised they might see more value in using me as a guinea pig—a notion equally unsettling.

They led me to an elevator. Limping, I braced for another grim ordeal similar to my previous capture—or perhaps something worse. Time stretched interminably: the scrape of my injured foot on concrete, the elevator's slow descent, one of the women prodding the lever with her baton, the other communicating tersely through her radio. The notion that I had journeyed this far only to be recaptured was a crushing realization. Exiting the elevator, we emerged into a spacious room dimly lit by two frosted windows that stretched from floor to ceiling along the inclined wall. Nestled between them was an imposing granite door. I inferred it to be the entrance hall.

My attention shifted to a group of women in red uniforms on the opposite side of the room. As we approached, another figure was led toward them, clad in the same yellow overalls I had been made to wear upon my first arrival in this world.

"La—" My voice faltered. Clearing my throat, I tried again, "Larissa?"

Her swollen eye, marred chin, and the gaps in her smile, where teeth once were, hinted at the cruelty she had endured. Tears streaked her face as she responded, her voice breaking, "Where are the others? Jacob and…?"

Overwhelmed by shame, I couldn't voice the reality. Instead, I shook my head somberly.

"I see," she whispered, looking downcast. "I'm sorry."

"What did they do to you?" I managed to ask.

She took a breath, "I'm fine now. They won't hurt me anymore."

A soldier approached, handing something to one of my captors—a radio transmitter, it seemed. The woman inspected it before passing it to me. Confusion swept over me, but somewhere deep down, a glimmer of understanding began to flicker.

"Why have they brought us here?" I asked. "What's happening?"

Larissa's voice was firm, "I struck a deal. It was our only chance."

"No," tears welled up in my eyes. "I won't leave you—"

My voice reverberated through the vast room, cut short by the distant wail of a child. As a unit of soldiers entered through a door, the heart-wrenching sound followed them. I clamped a hand over my mouth, tears breaking free and streaming down my face.

"Stay strong," Larissa urged. "I chose this."

"What are you saying?" I asked, frantically searching for the source of the cries.

Larissa sighed. "Jacob was right—they would never trade

something crucial to their cause unless we offered them something equally vital. But he was wrong too, Abasi. Advanced weaponry isn't the only game-changer in war. I've offered to teach them how to cure the plague, but only if they return your son and his mother to you."

"Son?" The word barely left my lips, choked out between sobs.

My emotions tore me in two directions—soaring joy collided with abject sorrow. As the soldiers aligned into formation, Dura emerged from behind them. A child was cradled in her arms, its soft cries filling the air. One look at his dark skin, and I knew he was ours. Dura moved beside me, lifting the boy so I could see his innocent face. A tumultuous wave of emotions washed over me; my body shook with joy and relief, even as my eyes brimmed with sorrow and regret. The bond I felt with the boy was immediate and profound, as if he were a piece of me I had lost when I cowardly left his mother by the cave. I yearned to hold him, to feel the softness of his skin against mine, but the stakes were too high to make such a move just yet.

"They've arranged a car for you outside," Larissa relayed. "Once you're safely in the valley, radio in to confirm you're okay. That's when I'll uphold my end of the deal."

"But you shouldn't be the one left behind," I protested. "I'm the reason—"

"Stop," she cut in softly. "This is where I need to be. I can help them. Healing, saving lives—that's what I do. And once I've aided them, I'll find a way to assist the Denisovans too."

The massive doors groaned open, their scraping reverberating through the room. A pungent aroma of burning rubber and smoldering buildings wafted in. Although the war had been momentarily pushed beyond the city walls, its traces were inescapable. I looked at Larissa's bruised face one last time.

"I hope fate allows our paths to cross again," I said.

Yet, deep down, we both sensed the finality of this parting. I was ushered outdoors alongside Dura and our child. A group of soldiers waited for us at the base of the pyramid's grand staircase. One of them held open the door to a sleek car. Though no one spoke, the stern expressions on their faces conveyed their displeasure at the terms they had grudgingly accepted.

I placed the radio in the backseat and settled into the driver's seat, my hands gripping the steering wheel. Dura sat beside me, our child in her arms. I found myself wrestling with the moral implications of bringing her back to my world, as opposed to reuniting her with the remnants of her own people. Ultimately, it was a moot point; she would never be safe in her world, not while caring for a child of such significance. I pressed down on the accelerator, the engine roaring to life, and we navigated through the war-torn city.

Buildings lay charred or in complete ruin. Desperate Neanderthals sifted through the debris, searching for loved ones. My heart ached for them, victims of choices made beyond their control. Further ahead, a group of Denisovan soldiers faced an imminent firing squad on a street corner. This was my first close look at their ranks. Adorned in white coats and green turbans, their faces bore the marks of defeat and illness. Yet, even in this dire moment, a hint of pride shone in their eyes.

No one paid us any attention as we drove through the streets. The city guards, after a brief communication from a higher authority, promptly let us through the gate. Beyond the city limits, we passed a procession of tanks mobilizing to fortify the city's defenses. After that, only the desolate road leading back to the valley lay before us. I cast a downward glance at my son, asleep in Dura's embrace. His face, a tranquil blend of our two worlds, bore Neanderthal traces, yet I couldn't envision him struggling to fit into my world. My heart swelled with love for him, but it was also shadowed by sorrow for those who had either perished or been forced to make monumental sacrifices, largely due to my actions. Each of them were heroes, with Larissa standing out as something even greater. I, on the other hand, was merely a father in search of redemption.

I turned to Dura. Her piercing gaze remained fixed on the path ahead, yet it was evident she was seeing something much further away—a world far beyond her imagination. I wondered if she would ever be able to truly adapt to it and lead a normal life. Emotions churned within me as I considered the challenges ahead. *Could she find a home, secure a job, or even discover love?* She deserved it all, but the journey would undoubtedly be fraught.

We reached the valley under the cover of night. Navigating the uneven terrain with our child was arduous, and upon finally arriving at the cave entrance I promptly radioed in. A Neanderthal responded, quickly passing the radio to Larissa when she realized it was me on the line. I assured her we hadn't been followed, as per their promise. Before the call was abruptly terminated, Larissa's voice came through: "I'll miss you... all of you."

Soon, she would be the last *Homo sapiens* in this realm.

Our child's cries reverberated through the cave as we maneuvered through its tight confines. It took us the entire night just to reach the midway chamber. The burden of carrying our small child through the claustrophobic labyrinth was even more grueling than I had anticipated, compounded by the lingering pain from my experiences within the pyramid. There were moments when I doubted our ability to make it through. However, as the first rays of morning light filtered through the cave's opening, a newfound strength surged within us, enabling us to cover the remaining hundred yards without succumbing to exhaustion. I clung to the hope that once we emerged into that light, our tribulations would truly be behind us.

"Welcome back," a voice greeted us as we struggled out of the cave's mouth and into my world's version of the valley. "Where's Jacob?"

A knot formed in my stomach, my heart plummeting. Dura clutched our son tightly. Jacob's final words echoed in my mind, now taking on a new and chilling clarity. *Swear to me—don't let 'em take you.* He hadn't meant the Neanderthals. The man addressing us wore a NATO uniform, though I couldn't discern his nationality. He took a drag from his cigar, eyeing Dura and our child with a mix of cruelty and curiosity. Behind him, soldiers in camouflage guarded a large military helicopter. Trees had been haphazardly cleared for its landing, further fueling my anger.

"Jacob didn't make it," I whispered. "He's gone."

The man responded with a hint of annoyance, "That's unfortunate. I was counting on his intel. Perhaps yours will suffice?"

Before I could fully process the situation, we found ourselves inside the helicopter—a terrifying metal beast from Dura's viewpoint. I could only guess at the terror she must've felt. They transported us to a secluded military compound, which served as a gateway to a network of fortified underground bunkers where we've been held ever since. They've dressed us in blue overalls marked with numbers across the chest. Though we're forbidden to leave, I've covertly dispatched these fragments of our tale with the aid of a compassionate private who visits every Sunday.

Every day has become monotonous, an endless loop. I wake up in my cell, and they drag me to an interrogation chamber, pressing me to divulge every facet of my journey to that alternate realm. They're tight-lipped about their intentions, but I've caught wind of corridor whispers hinting at tunnel construction. I fear they're gearing up for something—possibly an invasion.

I've arranged with the private aiding me to attach her contact number on a separate note. If you're willing, perhaps you can coordinate with her to devise a plan to help us. If that's too risky for you, I understand. However, please at least make my story known to the world. Publicizing it may thwart the military's nefarious plans for conquest.

Whatever course you choose, please act promptly. My concern for Dura and our child is escalating, as they're being subjected to tests that coldly assess their strengths and vulnerabilities, with little regard for their well-being. I've been attempting to devise a plan of my own to reach out to Dura and escape. However, she's perpetually monitored from behind an observation window and through the trails of the general's cigar smoke that rise to the ceiling like snakes chasing their own tails.

Sincerely,
Abasi Hamisi

POSTFACE

THIS BOOK SERVES AS a rallying cry for collective action, not only for my former student but also for Larissa and all those trapped by the oppressive regime beyond that mysterious cavern. I urge readers to think carefully before taking any hasty actions after reading this account. The insights within these pages require careful consideration, grounded in our democratic principles and values. We must tackle this issue as a united front; secretive actions by a few could lead to disaster. In keeping with Abasi's hopes, I've decided to bring this issue into the public eye—not as a signal for individual action but to ensure openness and encourage community involvement. Perhaps it would have been fortunate if the alternate realm had stayed hidden, but now that its existence is known to some, it's essential for it to be recognized by all.

I've communicated with the young woman assisting Abasi. She's committed to stepping forward as a whistle-blower if this chronicle garners public attention. Naturally, her individual efforts are not sufficient to counter potential plots against the parallel realm, but her firsthand account holds significant potential to inspire the public to take impactful action.

Through the collective voice of the public and the support

of institutions dedicated to upholding human rights for all, I am confident that there will be a push to release Abasi and his family, setting aside any invasive intentions. Consequently, we may usher in a new era of exploration rather than one of conquest—united in purpose as a singular species.

Nathalie Delsarte

About the Author

Tobias Malm has always possessed a penchant for exploring worlds beyond our own. Weaving intricate tales that draw from his myriad of personal interests—ranging from philosophy and science to his love for nature—Tobias creates narratives that captivate and provoke deep thought. When not lost in the labyrinth of his imagination, you might find him crafting intricate closed terrariums in jars, a reflection of his passion for contained ecosystems, or wandering through forests, deriving inspiration from the world around him.

The Cave To Another World is a testament to his flair for blending speculative fiction with immersive storylines that challenge our understanding of reality. It follows his previous work, *Julia Was A Special Girl And Other Unearthly Tales*, a riveting collection of speculative suspense stories that is a must-read for every fan of his most recent novel. If you enjoyed this journey through the alternate timelines and the profound twists of *The Cave To Another*

World, kindly consider leaving an honest review on Amazon or Goodreads. Your feedback helps authors like Tobias grow and bring more enthralling stories to readers like you.

Tobias invites you to delve deeper into his universe and stay updated with his latest projects. Connect with him through his official website www.tobiasmalm.com or show your support and get exclusive content by joining his community on Patreon at https://www.patreon.com/tobiasmalm. You can also find him on Instagram @malmtobias and Facebook facebook.com/malmtobias.

Thank you for journeying through this tale, and remember—there are always more caves to explore, more worlds to uncover, and more stories to be told.